HOOKY

MÍRIAM BONASTRE TUR

ETCH
CLARION BOOKS
IMPRINTS OF HARPERCOLLINS*PUBLISHERS*
BOSTON NEW YORK

A DIGITAL VERSION OF *HOOKY* WAS ORIGINALLY PUBLISHED ON WEBTOON IN 2015.

ETCH AND CLARION BOOKS ARE IMPRINTS OF HARPERCOLLINS PUBLISHERS.

CLARIONBOOKS.COM

THE TEXT WAS SET IN AMES PRO.

LETTERING BY NATALIE FONDRIEST

LIBRARY OF CONGRESS CATALOGING-IN-PUBLICATION DATA IS ON FILE.
ISBN: 978-0-358-46829-5 PAPERBACK
ISBN: 978-0-358-46830-1 HARDCOVER
ISBN: 978-0-358-66754-4 SIGNED EDITION
ISBN: 978-0-358-62343-4 B&N SIGNED EDITION

PRINTED IN CANADA
FSN 10 9 8 7 6 5 4 3 2
450083328

FIRST EDITION

CHAPTER 1

WAIT, DANI!
ARGH!
KIDS, DON'T RUN IN THE STREET!
HURRY, DORIAN.
STATION
CITY HALL
CASTLE
CEMETERY
WE'RE LATE!

OH NO—
THE BUS IS LEAVING!
I'M NOT GONNA ALLOW IT!
HERE WE GO!
HOP
THUD

COME ON...
FLY...
AH!
FINALLY.
HEY, WAIT FOR ME!
UGH...
YAY!

HOLD YOUR HORSES.
!
AH!
UGH...
OUCH.
OOF—ARE YOU OKAY?

DORIAN, WHAT ARE YOU DOING? WHY WOULD YOU GRAB MY BROOM?
SORRY. I DIDN'T THINK YOU'D FALL SO HARD.
MY HEAD HURTS NOW. AND I WAS SO CLOSE TO REACHING THE BUS!
BUT DANI, EVERYONE COULD SEE YOU.
WHAT IF THEY REALIZE WE'RE WITCHES?
WHAT IF THEY BURN US?
THAT WILL NEVER HAPPEN, DORIAN.
WE CAN FLY, REMEMBER?
OH, REALLY?
EVEN WHEN I'M CARRYING ALL *YOUR* BAGS?
OOPS. I WAS WONDERING WHY I WAS SO FAST...
...SORRY.
WHATEVER.
WE'VE GOT BIGGER PROBLEMS.
WE MISSED THE BUS AND DON'T KNOW WHERE THE SCHOOL IS.

MOM AND DAD WILL BE SO MAD WE MISSED THE BUS AND CAN'T GO TO SCHOOL THIS YEAR.
AHH!
IT'S IMPOSSIBLE TO FIND THE SCHOOL...
FOR SAFETY REASONS, NOBODY KNOWS WHERE IT IS.
I'M SURE THE BUS HAS ALREADY TELEPORTED.
OH NO!
WE'VE GOT TO FIND SOMEPLACE TO STAY FOR NINE MONTHS.
WE CAN'T GO HOME. IT'D BE A DISASTER.
YOU'RE RIGHT.
MOM AND DAD WILL KILL US!
WELL, DANI...
WE NEED A TUTOR.

CHAPTER 2

DANIELA AND DORIAN...
WHAT ARE YOU TWO DOING HERE?
G-GOOD AFTERNOON, AUNT HILDE.
SORRY FOR BOTHERING YOU THIS LATE, BUT...
DO YOU WANT TO BE OUR TUTOR?
YOU MUST KNOW THAT I RECEIVED YOU BECAUSE WE'RE FAMILY,
BUT I HAVE NO TIME FOR CHILDISH GAMES. I'M VERY BUSY.
JUST GIVE US SOME CHORES, WE'LL DO ANYTHING!
WE WON'T TAKE UP MUCH TIME.
DO YOUR PARENTS KNOW YOU'RE HERE?
SHOULDN'T YOU BE AT SCHOOL?

HUH? WELL—
YES, AUNT HILDE. THEY KNOW.
THEY SAID THAT INSTEAD OF GOING TO SUCH AN AVERAGE SCHOOL,
IT WOULD BE BETTER FOR OUR EDUCATION IF A BRILLIANT, BEAUTIFUL, AND ILLUSTRIOUS WITCH LIKE YOU COULD TEACH US.
THAT MAKES SENSE.
DON'T YOU WORRY, AUNTIE HILDE WILL TEACH YOU THE ART OF MAGIC.
I HAVE THE PERFECT CHORE.
YOU'LL START WORKING TOMORROW MORNING!
THIS...
...IS INSULTING.
SHE TRICKED US!

I'D LIKE TO KNOW WHY SOMEONE LIKE ME, ESTEEMED HEIR OF THE WYTTE FAMILY, IS DOING SERVANTS' WORK!
C'MON, DON'T BE LIKE THAT.
YOU SHOULD TAKE THE OPPORTUNITY TO PRACTICE WITH THE BROOM.
NO WAY!
WITH THIS PIECE OF JUNK, I'LL END UP CRASHING INTO THE SHELVES.
HAVE YOU SEEN ALL THESE BOOKS?
AT THIS RATE, YOU'LL NEVER FINISH.
HOW'S THIS FOR FAST?
HEY!
BE CAREFUL! YOU ALMOST HIT ME.
QUIT THROWING BOOKS AROUND.

JUST A SECOND...
...
AHA! HERE IT IS.
WATCH YOURSELF, DANI!
HERE WE GO...
WHOA,
THE BOOKS ARE MOVING!

AWESOME.

LET ME TRY!
LOOKS EASY.
AH!
UGH!
ACK!
OUCH!
WHY ISN'T IT WORKING? I USED THE SAME SPELL.
DORIAN, I'M COMING FOR YOU!

I'VE GOT YOU!
THANKS.
YOUR SPELL WAS SO COOL.
I KNOW.
THERE, WE'RE DONE.

AUNT HILDE IS GOING TO FREAK OUT WHEN SHE SEES WE'RE ALREADY FINISHED!
YEAH!
YOU WON'T BELIEVE IT, AUNT HILDE! WE'VE CLEANED UP THE LIBRARY.
YES, AND I USED A SUPER POWERFUL SPELL TO DO IT!
ALREADY?
YES! AREN'T YOU IMPRESSED?
IT WAS EASY PEASY. WE DESERVE A REWARD!
A REWARD, HUH?
FINE. I THINK I MIGHT HAVE UNDERESTIMATED YOU...
FOLLOW ME. I'M GOING TO GIVE YOU A MISSION WORTHY OF WYTTE'S HEIRS.
YAY!
SURE THING.
HERE.
HE'S BEEN LOCKED UP FOR A COUPLE OF DAYS.
I'M A VERY BUSY WOMAN...

...SO I HAVEN'T HAD THE TIME TO MOVE HIM.
HE'S OUR ENEMY.
AN ENEMY OF ALL WITCHES.
YOUR MISSION IS...
...TO TAKE HIM TO OUR PRISON.
NO PROBLEM.
LEAVE IT TO US!

UH...
AH!
DORIAN, STOP MOVING ALREADY!
I CAN'T!
IT'S NOT MY FAULT THIS BROOM IS DEFECTIVE.
SIGH...
I HAVE AN IDEA.
PLEASE
IN SEARCH OF APPRENTICES
...
I BET YOU DID SOMETHING AWFUL TO GET LOCKED UP.
DANI, GET ME OUT OF HERE! THIS DELINQUENT IS GIVING ME WEIRD LOOKS.
SOON. WE'RE ALMOST THERE.

SO, YOU'RE THE WYTTE TWINS...
THAT'S US!
IT'S A PLEASURE TO MEET YOU. YOUR PARENTS ARE EXEMPLARY WITCHES.
THEY'VE HELPED US A LOT WITH ALL THIS. YOUR AUNT HILDE, TOO.
ALL THIS?
YES... YOUR PRISONER IS THE LAST ONE. I'LL LET YOU IN ON OUR PLANS,
BUT YOU MUSTN'T TELL ANYONE.
A SECRET PLAN? COOL!
OUR LIPS ARE SEALED.
PERFECT.

WE'RE HEADING DOWN TO THE DUNGEONS. DON'T BE SCARED.
OF COURSE NOT.
DORIAN! ARE YOU COMING OR NOT?
YEP, COMING!
YOU'RE SO SPACEY TODAY.
I'M NOT SPACEY, I'M THOUGHTFUL!

CHAPTER 3

DANI!
ARE YOU THERE?
THIS IS SO DA—
AAARGH!
RUN, DORIAN.
YOU'RE GOING TO FALL BEHIND!
I'VE READ ABOUT THIS PRISON. THE SECURITY MEASURES ARE INTENSE.
THAT'S RIGHT. THIS PLACE HAS NO ESCAPE.
ONCE PRISONERS ARRIVE...
...THEY NEVER LEAVE.

POOR PRISONERS.
WHO ARE THEY?
DON'T PITY THEM.
THESE PEOPLE ARE AGAINST US.
THEY'RE ENEMIES OF ALL WITCHES.
LET'S GO, KIDS.
WE'RE DONE HERE.
THEY WON'T BE ABLE TO INTERFERE ANYMORE.
THIS BOY IS GOING TO ROT HERE, JUST LIKE THE OTHERS.
WAIT!
YOU—
YOU AND YOUR SISTER DON'T SEEM LIKE THE REST OF THEM.

LISTEN. DON'T TRUST ANYONE.
THEY'RE PLOTTING SOMETHING TERRIBLE.
THIS IS JUST THE FIRST STEP!
THEY'RE GOING TO—
DON'T TOUCH HIM!
DORIAN!
ARE YOU OKAY?
THAT WAS A MISTAKE, BOY.
AND IN VAIN.
THE WYTTES ARE RESPECTABLE WITCHES.
AND FROM NOW ON, YOU ARE NOTHING MORE THAN A PRISONER.
YOU MIGHT THINK IT'S ALL IN VAIN...

BUT WE'RE NOT DONE FIGHTING!
WHOA, DORIAN, THAT WAS FREAKY.
I GOT GOOSE BUMPS WHEN I SAW HIM GRAB YOU.
DON'T OVERREACT, DANI.
I'M NOT. IT WAS TERRIFYING!
WHO DOES HE THINK HE IS, SAYING THOSE THINGS?
HUH? WHAT THINGS?
WHAT THINGS?! HE SAID WE WEREN'T LIKE OTHER WITCHES!
BUT WE'RE AS GOOD AS THE REST!
RIGHT...
DORIAN, ARE YOU LISTENING TO ME?
...

SIR, COULD YOU WAIT A MOMENT, PLEASE?
WHERE ARE YOU GOING?
COME WITH ME!
CAN YOU GET YOUR BROOM?
YEAH, WHY?
KIDS THESE DAYS...
THEY HAVE WAY TOO MUCH ENERGY.
HERE IT IS!
SEARCHING FOR APPRENTICES
DORIAN, WHAT—?
SHHH, WAIT A SECOND! YOU'LL SEE.
NO!
STOP!
YOU'LL BURN YOURSELF!

CALM DOWN, I'VE GOT IT.
OKAY...
BUT WHAT DO YOU WANT THE EGG F—
HEY YOU!
PUT THAT BACK!
KIDS!
HURRY, DANI. THE BROOM!
I KNOW, I KNOW!
COME BACK HERE AT ONCE!
THIEVES!
SIR, WHAT DO WE DO?
I SEE... THE WYTTE FAMILY HAS BETRAYED US.

KNOCK THEM DOWN!
ATTACK, EVERYONE! FIRE AT WILL.
UH OH.
HEY, BE CAREFUL! YOU'RE GONNA TIP US OVER.
I THINK THEY'RE A LITTLE ANGRY...

NO, THE EGG!
WE DON'T HAVE TIME FOR THAT.
THEY'RE TRYING TO KNOCK US DOWN. HOLD ON TIGHT!
WHAT ARE YOU GONNA DO?
SAVE YOUR LIFE.
THIEVES!

THEY'RE ESCAPING.
WHERE'S THE EGG?
THEY'RE NOT CHASING US...
BECAUSE WE DON'T HAVE THE EGG.
LUCKILY, YOU DROPPED IT.
THAT'S NOT LUCKY AT ALL. IT'S A SHAME.
A SHAME?
WE ALMOST GOT KILLED BECAUSE OF YOU!
I DIDN'T KNOW THEY'D REACT LIKE THAT!
DORIAN...
IN MY OPINION, IT WAS A DISPROPORTIONATE REACTIO—
OH.

CHAPTER 4

DORIAN, ARE WE THERE YET?
NO.
ARE YOU SURE WE'RE HEADING IN THE RIGHT DIRECTION?
TO AUNT HILDE'S, YOU MEAN? NOPE.
HUH? THEN WHERE ARE WE—
IT WAS EITHER CATCH THIS TRAIN AT THE STATION WE FOUND...
OR KEEP WANDERING THROUGH THE WOODS.
PLATFORM I
IF ONLY WE HADN'T BROKEN THE BROOM...
THIS IS UNBELIEVABLE!
THE WYTTE FAMILY HEIRS, USING PUBLIC TRANSPORTATION LIKE COMMONERS.
WELL, WHOSE FAULT IS THAT?
NOT THIS AGAIN!
WELL, IT'S TRUE! WHEN WE GET HOME, WE'LL BE TOLD OFF BECAUSE OF YOU.

BUT IT WAS AMAZING—A DRAGON EGG!
AND WHAT WERE YOU GOING TO DO WITH IT?
SIT ON IT UNTIL IT HATCHED?
OF COURSE NOT. YOU NEED FIRE TO HATCH A DR—
!
WATCH OUT!
A BALL?
THAT WAS A CLOSE CALL.
AHA! HERE IT IS, GUYS.
GRAB IT, NICO.
BEFORE THE GUARD CATCHES US!
WE'RE LUCKY IT BOUNCED OFF THE WINDOW!!
LUCKY?
YOU NEARLY TOOK MY HEAD OFF!
FORTUNATELY, I SAVED HER LIFE WITH MY ASTONISHING REFLEXES.

REALLY?
WELL, THESE THINGS HAPPEN.
WHAT?!
DON'T BE MAD.
HOW RUDE!
CALM DOWN, DANI...
C'MON, IT WAS AN ACCIDENT...
HUH...
AHA!
YOU TWO!
PENDRAGON'S BEEN LOOKING FOR YOU FOR DAYS.
COME WITH ME!

HEY, BRAT!
YOU AREN'T LEAVING WITHOUT PAYING FOR THE BROKEN WINDOW, PUNK.
DO YOU TRUST THIS GUY, DORIAN?
HOW CRUEL. ASKING FOR MONEY FROM A DEFENSELESS KID.
DEFENSELESS? YOU? YOU'LL PAY THIS TIME, NICO.
I SEE...
IN THAT CASE, I'LL BE FORCED TO TELL YOUR WIFE ABOUT YOUR GAMBLING HABIT...
...FINE. GET OUT OF HERE.
THANKS, MAN. SEE YOU AROUND!
HE LOOKS LIKE THE TYPE OF GUY TO STEAL FROM YOU THE MINUTE YOUR BACK IS TURNED.
HE SEEMS FUN.
LET'S GO.
WHAT'S HE DOING NOW?
I DON'T KNOW...
READY...
SET...
GO!
WHERE ARE YOU GOING?

HEY! YOU'RE CATCHING UP TO ME.
DUH!
I'M EXHAUSTED... I'M NOT MADE FOR ATHLETICS.
YOU... YOU BARELY KEPT UP.
B... BUT WHAT'S THE HURRY?
WHY WALK WHEN WE CAN RACE?
LIFE'S TOO SHORT TO WASTE TIME WALKING.
... ARE YOU SERIOUS?
HUH?
AND JUST LOOK...
...WE'RE HERE.
THIS IS THE HOUSE OF MASTER PENDRAGON, THE SOOTHSAYER.

A SOOTHSAYER LIVES HERE? A WITCH?
HOW LAME...
DORIAN! SHUT UP, HE MIGHT FIGURE OUT WHO WE ARE!
AH... OOPS. I MEANT—
DON'T WORRY! I ALREADY KNOW IT ALL.
I WAS THE MASTER'S ASSISTANT ONCE, BUT I LEFT.
BUT DON'T YOU WORRY, YOU SEEM JUST AS WEIRD AS HE IS. YOU'LL GET ALONG.
I LEARNED TO RIDE A BROOM FROM HIM!
JUST A BIT, THOUGH.
REALLY?
YEP!
AND FROM THE STATE OF YOUR BROOM,
YOU MIGHT NEED SOME LESSONS.
WATCH IT, OR I'LL TURN YOU INTO A SLUG!
IF YOU'RE AS GOOD AT MAGIC AS YOU ARE AT FLYING, I DOUBT IT.
CHILDREN...
PLEASE, KEEP IT DOWN.
WELL, THERE HE IS! I'LL LEAVE YOU IN HIS HANDS.
'TIL NEXT TIME.
COME, CHILDREN...
I'VE BEEN EXPECTING YOU.

YOU'RE FINALLY HERE!
YOU TOOK YOUR TIME.
DIDN'T YOU SEE MY SIGNS?
UH... NO. SORRY...
I HAVE SO MANY THINGS TO TELL YOU.
BUT FIRST...
WOULD YOU LIKE SOME TEA?
I'D RATHER HAVE HOT CHOCOLATE...
YES, HOT CHOCOLATE, PLEASE!
HOT CHOCOLATE IT IS.
HERE YOU GO.
THANKS!
LET'S GET STRAIGHT TO THE POINT.
AS YOU KNOW, THE WORLD OF MAGIC REMAINS SECRET, EVEN TODAY.
PEOPLE BELIEVE WITCHES ARE A THING OF THE PAST.
YUCK, THIS TASTES WEIRD...
WITCHES MAKE AN EFFORT TO...
YEAH, KIND OF LIKE TEA.
...LAY LOW AND BE GOOD CITIZENS.
BUT...
MAN, I REALLY WANTED HOT CHOCOLATE.

THIS IS ALL I'VE GOT.
OOH, YUM!
THANK YOU.
AS I WAS SAYING, WE HAVE A PROBLEM.
A COMMUNITY OF EVIL WITCHES IS THREATENING TO BREAK OUR SILENCE.
THEY BEHAVE LIKE VILLAINS FROM FAIRY TALES.
THEY'RE CAPTURING AND IMPRISONING PEOPLE,
BREEDING MAGICAL CREATURES ILLEGALLY,
AND TAKING ADVANTAGE OF THEIR MAGIC TO LIVE IN LUXURY...
WHAT?
BUT THAT'S...
...TERRIBLE!
COMPLETELY UNACCEPTABLE!
HOW CAN PEOPLE DO SUCH THINGS?
I KNOW, I KNOW...
IT'S HORRIBLE.
THAT'S WHY I, MASTER PENDRAGON,
NEED YOUR HELP TO DEFEND THE HONOR OF ALL WITCHES.
I WILL TAKE YOU ON AS APPRENTICES.
DANI, DORIAN...
YOUR TRAINING BEGINS TODAY!
...
COOL.
SLURP

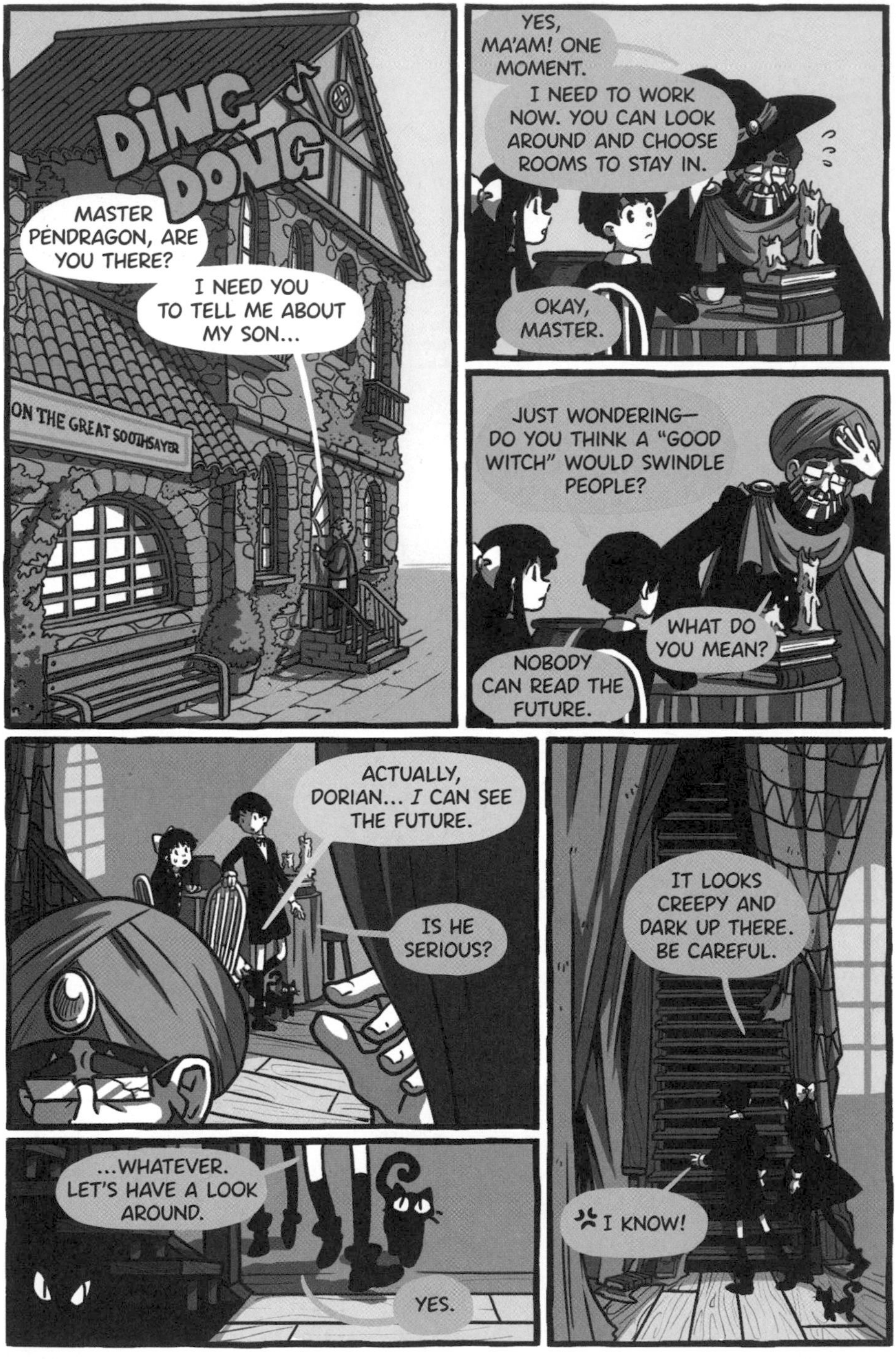
DING DONG
MASTER PENDRAGON, ARE YOU THERE?
I NEED YOU TO TELL ME ABOUT MY SON...
ON THE GREAT SOUTHSAYER
YES, MA'AM! ONE MOMENT.
I NEED TO WORK NOW. YOU CAN LOOK AROUND AND CHOOSE ROOMS TO STAY IN.
OKAY, MASTER.
JUST WONDERING— DO YOU THINK A "GOOD WITCH" WOULD SWINDLE PEOPLE?
WHAT DO YOU MEAN?
NOBODY CAN READ THE FUTURE.
ACTUALLY, DORIAN... *I* CAN SEE THE FUTURE.
IS HE SERIOUS?
...WHATEVER. LET'S HAVE A LOOK AROUND.
YES.
IT LOOKS CREEPY AND DARK UP THERE. BE CAREFUL.
I KNOW!

LOOK HOW POWERFUL I AM!
OOOH!
WHAT A BEAUTIFUL VIEW.
WHOA! A HIDDEN LIBRARY...

THE BIG LIST OF
EMENT'S MONSTERS
with people,
only way
It's important to be
DORIAN!
WHAT?
I FOUND MY ROOM!
OOOH...
TAP HUFF TAP HUFF TAP HUFF TAP TAP
WHAT DO YOU MEAN—
IT'S PRETTY NICE, RIGHT? HEHE!
LOOK, THERE'S A LITTLE LIBRARY! A COZY NOOK TO RELAX AND READ BOOKS IN.
TOO BAD I DON'T READ MORE—
AAAAAH
YOU'LL SEE! I'LL FIND AN EVEN BETTER ROOM.
WITH A *BETTER* LIBRARY!
GOOD LUCK!

SO... MANY... STAIRS...
AT THIS RATE, I'LL CHOOSE THE BASEMENT TO STAY IN.
WAIT.
WHAT IS...
...THIS?
BUMP
WHOA.

THIS ROOM IS AMAZING!
ARE YOU SURE YOU DON'T WANT TO SWITCH?
OF COURSE NOT!
IT'S MY SECRET LAIR NOW.
DO YOU THINK WE SHOULD STAY HERE?
WHY NOT?
DO YOU TRUST MASTER PENDRAGON?
HE SEEMS HARMLESS.
AND WE CAN'T GO HOME NOW. IF MOM AND DAD FIND OUT WE'VE MISSED THIS MUCH SCHOOL...
I KNOW... THEY CAN BE SCARY.
YEAH... PLUS, THERE'S... YOU KNOW WHO... THAT OTHER PERSON—
I KNOW.
DORIAN. ENOUGH.
YOUR NIECE AND NEPHEW TRIED TO STEAL A DRAGON EGG!
THEY WERE PROBABLY KIDDING AROUND.
THEY'RE CHILDREN.
THAT'S NO EXCUSE, HILDE.
IT WAS A DIRECT THREAT TO OUR PLANS.
THEY'RE *TRAITORS.*
SIGH... HOW TIRESOME.
I'VE FUNDED YOUR PLANS FROM THE BEGINNING.
I WILL NOT BE ASSOCIATED WITH TREASON.
FINE.
I'LL FIND THE CHILDREN AND SEE FOR MYSELF.
I OWE YOUR BROTHER A VISIT.
DO WHAT YOU WANT.

CHAPTER 5

GOOD MORNING, EVERYONE!
GOOD MORNING.
HEY.
YOU WOKE UP EARLY TODAY, DORIAN.
OF COURSE. I'M EAGER TO START CLASSES.
ARE YOU STUDYING?
NOPE.
I'M WRITING A LETTER TO MOM AND DAD.
I'M TELLING THEM THAT WE'RE AT SCHOOL.
GOOD IDEA! TELL THEM THAT WE ACED OUR FIRST TEST.
OKAY. I'LL PUT THAT WE'VE MADE A LOT OF FRIENDS, TOO.
AND OUR TEACHERS ARE IMPRESSED WITH OUR SKILLS.
I'M SURE MASTER *WILL* BE IMPRESSED SOON, AFTER ALL.
WHAT KIND OF LESSONS DO WE HAVE TODAY?
I WAS ACTUALLY THINKING WE COULD CLEAN THE HOUSE FIRST.
WHAT?!
NO WAY!
I CAN'T BELIEVE IT...
WE HAVEN'T LEARNED A SINGLE SPELL SINCE WE LEFT HOME.
ALL WE DO IS CLEAN.
WE CAN USE A SPELL TO CLEAN, IF YOU WANT.
HERE IT IS! THE HOUSEWORK MAGIC BOOK.
ME! ME!
LET ME TRY!
To fix objects
LET'S SEE...
For general
AAAARGH!
WHOA!
OH MY—

QUICK, WATER!
BACK UP, DANIELA.
AAH!
KIDS, LET'S CLEAN IN THE TRADITIONAL WAY.
ENOUGH MAGIC FOR TODAY.
WE CAN SPLIT UP THE WORK. DORIAN, YOU START WITH THE BATHROOM.
SIGH...
I'M A DISGRACE TO THE WYTTE FAMILY.
WHY CAN'T I DO ANY SPELLS PROPERLY?
I'M A MESS.
HEY, YOU!
OH NO... *HIM* AGAIN.
I HAVE TO TALK TO YOU.
LISTEN, DOROTHY—
DANI.
WHATEVER.
TELL ME, DANI...
YOU'RE A WITCH, RIGHT?
CAN YOU DO MAGIC AND STUFF?
OF COURSE I CAN DO MAGIC.
THANK GOODNESS.
I NEED YOUR HELP WITH SOMETHING REALLY IMPORTANT...

UGH...
EVANS CAFE
I CAN'T BELIEVE I'M HERE.
WHY ON EARTH DID I AGREE TO HELP THAT DUMMY?
THIS MORNING WE ACCIDENTALLY CRASHED A TOY PLANE INTO THE WINDOW OF EVANS CAFÉ.
MR. EVANS IS SCARY, BUT HIS EVIL SON, MARK, IS EVEN WORSE.
HE'S A BULLY!
AND WHY WOULD I HELP YOU?
PLEASE, I'LL DO WHATEVER YOU WANT IN RETURN, DIANE!
OKAY, FROM NOW ON YOU WILL CALL ME "QUEEN DANI."
DEAL!
SO... HERE I AM.
AND I HAVE NO IDEA HOW I'M GOING TO DO THIS.
THERE'S MR. EVANS...
AND THAT BOY MUST BE HIS SON, MARK.
AHA! AND THERE'S THE TOY PLANE!

HELLO, MISS. WHAT WOULD YOU LIKE TO EAT?
ACK!
UM... WELL...
THIS THING RIGHT HERE, PLEASE.
I DIDN'T EVEN HAVE TIME TO LOOK AT THE MENU.
WHAT IS SHE DOING?
I... I DON'T KNOW.
WHY DID YOU ASK HER TO DO THIS, NICO?
YEAH, WHAT CAN SHE DO THAT WE CAN'T?
COME ON, DAISY...
LET ME SEE!
HERE'S YOUR RAISIN BREAD PUDDING.
WHOA, THIS LOOKS DELICIOUS.
MUNCH
YUCK
THIS PUDDING IS *GROSS*.
I... I MEAN...
THIS PUDDING IS GROSSLY DELICIOUS. I LOVE IT!
REALLY?
I'LL BRING YOU MORE, THEN.
OH NO.
THIS MISSION... IS WAY HARDER THAN I THOUGHT.

IT'S IMPOSSIBLE.
I CAN'T FIND THE RIGHT SPELL.
AND I'VE EATEN *SO* MUCH OF THIS DISGUSTING PUDDING.
I SHOULD'VE STAYED AT MASTER'S HOUSE TO CLEAN.
IDEAS:
WAIT A MINUTE!
CLEANING...
THIS MORNING I...
...SWEAR I SAW A SPELL TO FIX OBJECTS IN THAT BOOK.
To fix objects
For general cleaning
IF I CAN FIX THE PLANE...
...NICO WILL BE ABLE TO MAKE IT FLY WITH THE REMOTE CONTROL.
IT HAS TO WORK!
WHAT WAS THAT?
SHHH!
HUH...
WHY ISN'T IT WORKING?
S CAFE
BOOM
WHOAAA!

RUN!
WHAT THE...?
MY HOUSE!
AAAGH!
...
AAARGH!
SOMEONE CALL THE FIREFIGHTERS.
WHAT IS THIS?
I DON'T GET IT.
DANI!
I SAID THE SPELL PERFECTLY.
SO WHY—
WATCH OUT!
WHY DOES EVERYTHING I DO GO WRONG?
CRASH

OH NO...
THIS IS WILD.
WHAT A DISAST—
EH?
AH.
SORRY, I COMPLETELY FORGOT ABOUT YOU.
HE LOOKS...
ARE YOU OKAY?
...LIKE A PRINCE.
HEY THERE...
ARE YOU LISTENING?
HUH?
NO, DON'T WORRY. I'M FINE.
PHEW, THAT'S A RELIEF.
I DON'T WANT ANYTHING TO HAPPEN TO A CUSTOMER.
NO, NO, OF COURSE I'M OKAY.
WHICH REMINDS ME...

...WHAT?
YOU HAVEN'T PAID. THE RAISIN BREAD PUDDINGS, REMEMBER?
AH.
I TOTALLY FORGOT.
I HAVE NO MONEY.
YOU IDIOT!
SLAP!
AAH!
OUCH! WHAT WAS THAT FOR, DAD?
I CAN'T BELIEVE YOU'RE ASKING THIS YOUNG LADY FOR MONEY.
OF COURSE. SHE'S A CUSTOMER!
YES, AND SHE ALMOST DIED IN AN EXPLOSION AT OUR ESTABLISHMENT!
TODAY IS ON THE HOUSE.
COME ON, MARK, APOLOGIZE TO THE YOUNG LADY.
...OKAY.
I'M SORRY.
WHAT?!
YOU'RE MARK EVANS?
EV
B... BUT... THEN WHO'S THAT BOY?
BOB? HE'S A NEIGHBOR AND A CUSTOMER. WHY DO YOU ASK?
UH... NO REASON.
LET'S GET BACK TO WORK, MARK. WE HAVE TO CLEAN UP THIS MESS.

LET'S SEE THE CAUSE OF ALL THIS.
THE PLANE IS A TOY AGAIN!
SO HE'S NICO'S BULLY...
I GUESS I'LL SEND THE BILL TO OLD MAN PENDRAGON.
MASTER PENDRAGON? I LIVE WITH HIM!
REALLY?
BUT YOU SEEM SO NORMAL.
HE'S A LITTLE SCARY...
BUT ALSO CUTE.
YOU'RE NEW IN TOWN, RIGHT?
YOU'LL SEE HOW STRANGE THINGS ARE AROUND HERE. IT'S ALWAYS PENDRAGON.
BUT HE'S A GOOD GUY, I THINK.
HEY MARK—
CAN YOU GIVE ME THE TOY PLANE?
BUT IT'S BROKEN.
YES! COME ON, DANI.
PLEASE? I'LL EVEN PAY FOR THE PUDDINGS.
I DON'T MIND.
IT'S JUST JUNK. HAVE AT IT.
BY THE WAY, WHAT'S YOUR NA—
SEE YOU, MARK!
SORRY FOR THE INCONVENIENCE.
ER, BYE.
I DID IT! I RECOVERED THE PLANE!
I'M NOT A COMPLETE DISASTER AFTER ALL!
GOOD JOB, CAPTAIN DANI.
I DON'T UNDERSTAND WHAT HAPPENED, BUT YAY!
THE PLANE IS TOTALLY BROKEN, THOUGH.
I CAN FIX IT, DON'T WORRY.
ARE YOU SURE?
TRUST ME, NICO. I KNOW EXACTLY WHAT TO DO.

DORIAN!
ARE YOU THERE?
AH!
WHAT IS HE DOING ALL ALONE IN THE DARK?
WHAT A WEIRDO.
I KNEW YOU WOULD BE HERE!
WHAT ARE YOU DOING?
NOTHING! I'M NOT HIDING ANYTHING AT ALL!
DO YOU REMEMBER THAT FIXING SPELL FROM THIS MORNING?
Y-YES, I DO.
CAN YOU FIX THIS?
PLEASE, MY LOVELY BROTHER?
SURE!
THAT'S IT? HOW BORING.
JUST GIVE ME A SECOND.
YAY!
WHOAAAA!
DORIAN MAKES IT LOOK SO EASY... I GUESS I SHOULD STUDY.
WOW! THIS IS AMAZING!
I KNOW, I KNOW.
THANK YOU SO MUCH, DANI!
DON'T MENTION IT. BUT REMEMBER—
HUH?
OH, YES, SORRY! QUEEN DANI, I MEAN.
THAT'S BETTER.
LET'S GET OUT OF HERE. THIS PLACE REEKS OF OLD BOOKS.
BUT... WAIT...

CHAPTER 6
THE PRINCE HAS BEEN KIDNAPPED!
WE NEED TO FIND HIM IMMEDIATELY.
AND WITCHES SHOULD BE ELIMINATED ONCE AND FOR ALL!
CALM DOWN, PLEASE.
WE ARE DOING EVERYTHING WE CAN.
I'VE SENT MANY SOLDIERS, BUT—
I WON'T CALM DOWN, GEORGE.
WILLIAM IS MY SON! AND HE'S BEEN KIDNAPPED UNDER YOUR ROOF!
HOW DO YOU PLAN TO FIX IT?!
HE COULD HAVE BEEN KIDNAPPED ANYWHERE.
THE WITCHES HAVE BEEN SNATCHING PRINCES FROM NEIGHBORING KINGDOMS, TOO.
IF YOU'LL ALLOW ME...: MY WIFE HAS A POINT.
WE SHOULD HAVE BURNED THE WITCHES AT THE STAKE WHEN WE HAD THE CHANCE.
I NEVER UNDERSTOOD THIS MERCY FROM YOU.
THEN WE WOULDN'T HAVE THIS PROBLEM NOW.
POOR WILLIAM... I HOPE HE'S ALL RIGHT.
GO SEE HOW MONICA FEELS.
YES, YOUR MAJESTY.

YOUR DAUGHTER IS A USELESS CRYBABY.
I HEARD SHE HASN'T LEFT HER ROOM SINCE WILLIAM DISAPPEARED.
MY POOR DAUGHTER IS HAVING A VERY HARD TIME!
POOR PRINCESS... SHE'S BEEN LYING THERE FOR DAYS...
SHE MUST BE EXHAUSTED FROM ALL THE CRYING.
WELL, PRINCE WILLIAM IS HER FIANCÉ.
TWO LOVERS SEPARATED BY DESTINY... SUCH A TRAGEDY! SO ROMANTIC!
SHHH, SHE'S GONNA HEAR US.
YOU MUST NOT HAVE MUCH WORK IF YOU'RE WASTING TIME SPYING ON THE PRINCESS.
AAAAH!
COME ON, PRINCESS... CHEER UP.
THE PRINCE IS MISSING, BUT YOU HAVE US.
WE'RE HERE FOR WHATEVER YOU NEED.
IT BREAKS MY HEART TO SEE YOU LIKE THIS. MY MAKEUP IS RUINED FROM CRYING FOR YOU.
LET'S GO SHOPPING! IT ALWAYS CHEERS YOU UP.
ALSO, I NEED A NEW PAIR OF SHOES.
COME ON, YOU CAN'T JUST SIT HERE ALL DAY LONG!
YOU'RE RIGHT.
OF COURSE WE ARE.
I CAN'T STAY HERE ANY LONGER.
I HAVE TO SAVE HIM.

I'M HIS FIANCÉE.
ENOUGH HIDING LIKE A HELPLESS MAIDEN. I'M A STRONG AND CAPABLE WOMAN!
YOU'RE FOURTEEN, PRINCESS.
IT'S MY DUTY TO SAVE WILLIAM AND BRING HIM HOME, SAFE AND SOUND.
I'LL DEFEAT THE EVIL WITCHES, RISKING MY LIFE IF NECESSARY.
IT WILL BE DANGEROUS AND BLOODY. WE MIGHT NOT ALL MAKE IT.
BUT IN THE END, WHEN I'VE RESCUED HIM, MY BELOVED WILLIAM AND I...
...WILL FINALLY GET MARRIED.
THEY'LL ERECT A STATUE IN MY HONOR AND EVERYTHING. I'LL BE A HEROINE.
HO HO HO!
BUT DON'T WORRY, GIRLS, I KNOW I CAN COUNT ON YOU. YOU'LL BE BY MY SIDE EVERY STEP OF THE WAY.
HUH... NOW THAT I THINK ABOUT IT...
WE'D JUST GET IN THE WAY!
GOOD LUCK ON YOUR ADVENTURES, PRINCESS!
HEY, GIRLS. WAIT!
GIRLS?
WHATEVER. I DON'T NEED ANYONE.
I NEED TO LAY LOW, ANYWAY.
I'LL ONLY TAKE THE ESSENTIALS.
PLUS A WEAPON TO DEFEND MYSELF.

I'M READY FOR MY MISSION.
WAIT FOR ME, BELOVED WILLIAM. I'M COMING FOR YOU!
WOW, THIS IS SO FUN.
I'VE NEVER TAKEN A TRAIN BEFORE.
I FEEL LIKE PART OF THE RIFFRAFF.
EXCUSE ME, YOUNG LADY, BUT ARE YOU PRINCESS MONICA?
YES, I AM!
I'VE EMBARKED ON A ROMANTIC QUEST TO FIND SOMEONE.
BUT TO BE HONEST, I DON'T KNOW WHERE TO START...
WELL, COME TO THINK OF IT...
...MY STOP IS NEXT. WE HAVE AN EXCELLENT SOOTHSAYER IN TOWN. MAYBE HE CAN HELP YOU?
SPLENDID! THANK YOU FOR THE GUIDANCE.
SOLDIERS, SHOW HER MY GRATITUDE.
PRINCESS, ARE YOU SURE THIS IS A GOOD IDEA?
OF COURSE! HAVEN'T YOU EVER READ AN ADVENTURE NOVEL?
MEETING THE MENTOR IS AN ESSENTIAL STEP ON ANY HEROINE'S JOURNEY.

I—I'M RICH!
WHAT'S ALL THIS ABOUT?
PRINCESS MONICA'S IN TOWN. SHE'S GIVING MONEY TO ANYONE WHO HELPS HER FIND PENDRAGON.
THAT'S IT?!
SEE YOU GUYS LATER!
GOOD MORNING, DEAR SUBJECTS.
YES, I'M THE PRINCESS. BUT DON'T SPREAD THE WORD, I'M ON A SECRET MISSION.
HEY!
I'M NICO, THE OFFICIAL TOWN GUIDE. I'M EXPENSIVE BUT RELIABLE.
I'M SORRY, I DON'T HAVE TIME TO SIGN AUTOGRAPHS.
MASTER PENDRAGON THE SOOTHSAYER IS A FRIEND OF MINE.
IF YOU LIKE, I CAN INTRODUCE YOU. AS I SAID, MY SERVICES ARE FIRST CLASS.
PERFECT— WILL THIS COVER IT?
B-BUT...
...THIS IS A FORTUNE!
HOHOHO
MONEY IS NO OBJECT, NICO.
WHAT IS NICO DOING? AND WHO'S THAT GIRL MAKING A RACKET?
KEEP WORKING, SLACKER!
COME ON, MASTER'S HOUSE IS THIS WAY.

MY DEAR APPRENTICES...
...I KNOW YOU'VE BEEN WAITING FOR SOME TIME NOW.
NOW, PAY ATTENTION.
BECAUSE TODAY IS THE DAY.
FINALLY I, MASTER PENDRAGON,
AM GOING TO TEACH YOU COMPLEX AND POWERFUL MAGICAL ARTS FOR DEFEATING EVIL.
OBSERVE! MY INCREDIBLE POW—
MAAASTERRRR! ARE YOU HOOOOME?!
—ER...
IS THAT NICO?
PRINCESS MONICA HAS COME TO SEE YOU. OPEN THE DOOR, MASTER!
HE CAN'T BE SERIOUS.
HOW EXCITING TO MEET THE PRINCESS!
RELAX, DANI. I'M AN EXPERT IN ROYAL ETIQUETTE.
OOH, REALLY?
I'VE READ LOADS ABOUT IT. WATCH AND LEARN.
COME ON, MASTER, WE MUST WELCOME THE PRINCESS.
WAIT, KIDS! IT COULD BE A TRAP!
WELCOME TO OUR HUMBLE ABODE, PRINCESS MONICA.

MY APOLOGIES FOR RECEIVING YOU IN A RESIDENCE SO UNDESERVING OF YOUR EXCELLENCE.
PLEASE ALLOW ME TO INTRODUCE MYSELF.
I AM DORIAN.
HEIR OF THE RENOWNED AND HONO—
AWW!
WHAT A CUTE KID.
HOLD ON TO MY SUITCASE, IT'S SO HEAVY...
AH?!
YOUR HOME IS SO CHARMING. WHAT LOVELY DÉCOR.
NOW, WHERE IS THE SOOTHSAYER?
ARE YOU LOOKING FOR ME, PRINCESS?
HEY, MASTER, GUESS WHAT? I'M RICH!
ARE YOU PENDRAGON?
I'VE BEEN INFORMED THAT YOU CAN SEE THE FUTURE.
THAT'S RIGHT. I'M THE BEST SOOTHSAYER ALIVE.
PERFECT! I NEED MY FUTURE TOLD. I'LL PAY WHATEVER IT TAKES.
FOLLOW ME.
SO, TELL ME...
WHAT IS YOUR QUESTION?

MY FIANCÉ, PRINCE WILLIAM, HAS BEEN KIDNAPPED BY WITCHES.
I WANT TO SAVE HIM.
I THOUGHT A SOOTHSAYER LIKE YOURSELF COULD HELP ME GET STARTED.
OF COURSE.
LET'S SEE WHAT THE CRYSTAL BALL TELLS US.
HMM... THE BALL IS SHOWING ME SOMETHING...
I SEE...
...A VERY HIGH TOWER. YOU'VE BEEN LOCKED IN. IT'S DARK...
A FULL MOON IN THE SKY, WHITE ROSES, ASHES AND FIRE. BUT REVERSED.
THE ASHES FIRST.
THEN THE FIRE.
I DON'T LIKE THIS AT ALL.
BUT IT'S THE TRUTH.
AND THERE'S SOMETHING ELSE... IT'S ABOUT YOUR PRINCE.
THE ONLY WAY TO FIND HIM IS TO STAY HERE...
...WITH US.
ATTENTION, EVERYONE!
I HAVE A VERY IMPORTANT ANNOUNCEMENT TO MAKE.

AFTER MUCH THOUGHT...
...AND UNDER THE GUIDANCE OF GRANDMASTER PENDRAGON...
...I'M STAYING HERE!
WHAT?!
WHY WOULD YOU STAY HERE, PRINCESS?
THE SOOTHSAYER SAYS THAT HE AND HIS APPRENTICES ARE PREPARING A PLAN TO DEFEAT THE EVIL WITCHES WHO KIDNAPPED WILL.
CLEARLY WE HAVE AN ENEMY IN COMMON.
BUT PRINCESS, THE OLD MAN'S PREDICTIONS ARE QUACKERY.
WE CAN'T TRUST THESE PEOPLE.
WELL, I'M THE ONLY ONE STAYING. I DON'T WANT TO BE A BURDEN TO THESE PEOPLE.
THAT'S EVEN WORSE!
WE CAN'T LEAVE YOU HERE ALONE. IT'S DANGEROUS.
HAVE YOU SEEN THIS MAN'S APPRENTICES?
THEY'RE LITTLE KIDS! THEY AREN'T DANGEROUS.
LOOK AT THIS. THEY EVEN HAVE A LITTLE KITTY CAT AS A PET!
WHAT'S HIS NAME?
...WE CALL HIM CAT.

I CAN'T BELIEVE YOU DIDN'T NAME YOUR CAT. SHAME ON YOU, PRINCESS DANI.
OOH, ARE YOU A PRINCESS TOO? FROM WHICH KINGDOM?
NO, I'M NOT A PRINCESS! NICO THINKS HE'S FUNNY, THAT'S ALL.
NOW THAT I THINK ABOUT IT, IT WOULD BE GREAT TO CREATE A PRINCESS RESCUERS CLUB!
THIS IS YOUR PRIZE, PRINCESS DANI. WE AGREED!
WELL, I DON'T WANT IT ANYMORE. CALL ME DANI!
ARE YOU SURE, SUPREME RULER?
DANI!
BUT THAT *WOULD* MEAN SHARING THE LIMELIGHT...
COME ON, CARLO, GO BACK INTO YOUR BOX.
DON'T BITE ME.
STOOOOP! CARLO!
ARGH!
WHAT—
PRINCESS, GET BEHIND ME.
DORIAN!
BUT WHA—
WHAT IS THAT?!
UH...

SORRY.
ARE YOU OKAY, DORIAN?
WHAT IS THAT UGLY THING?
WHERE DID YOU GET THAT FROM?
I'M SORRY, MASTER!
AFTER WHAT HAPPENED AT THE PRISON, I COULDN'T STOP THINKING ABOUT THE DRAGON EGG.
SO I READ ABOUT THEM, AND LEARNED ABOUT FIRE TONGUE FROGS.
YOU CAN RAISE THEM IN BASEMENTS.
SO YOU'VE BEEN RAISING HIM IN SECRET?
YES!
HAHA.
BUT IT'S NOT A *REAL* DRAGON.
A FIRE-SPITTING FROG? LAME!
SHUT UP, NICO, YOU'RE JUST JEALOUS.
JEALOUS? ME? LOOK AT HIS STUPID FACE!
AND THE FROG'S FACE LOOKS STUPID, TOO.
...
PRINCESS, ARE YOU OKAY?
UM...
SHE LOOKS SHOCKED.
I DON'T GET IT.
HOW CAN THAT FROG SPIT FIRE?
BASIC SPELLS
OTIONS
WAIT...
WHAT'S ALL THIS?
AND THAT?
OH NO.
IT CAN'T BE...
YOU...

...ARE WITCHES?
THESE PEOPLE ARE WITCHES!
SEIZE THEM!
HEY, WAIT A MINUTE. THIS IS A MISUNDERSTANDING!
STAY BACK, OLD MAN. AND NO FUNNY BUSINESS.
OLD MAN? YOU'RE NOT EXACTLY YOUNG, EITHER!
WHAT DID YOU WANT WITH THE PRINCESS? TO TAKE HER PRISONER?
HANDS OFF, DUDE!
NO SUDDEN MOVEMENTS, FROG BOY.
DORIAN—
DON'T TOUCH MY BROTHER!
KEEP STILL, LITTLE GIRL.
UGH!
HEY!
POW
STEP ASIDE!
THUMP
AGH!
GO EASY, HE'S JUST A KID.
WHAM
DON'T BE RIDICULOUS—THEY'RE WITCHES. THEY MUST BE BURNED!
NOW...

OOH...
GET OUT.
OR YOU'LL BE SORRY.
H-HE'S THREATENING ME!
CREEPY.
AMAZING!
CAN IT BE HIM?
WE'LL BE BACK!

WAIT—
PRINCESS!
WHAT?! LET ME GO!
PLEASE, LISTEN TO ME...
...DIDN'T YOU SAY THAT YOU WANTED TO SAVE YOUR PRINCE?
THEN YOU CAN'T GIVE UP ON THE FIRST TRY!
WHAT THE MASTER SAID IS TRUE...
...WE'RE WORKING AGAINST THE EVIL WITCHES!
WE HAVEN'T HURT ANYONE—
IT WAS *YOU* WHO ATTACKED US!
WHO ARE YOU TO DECIDE WE'RE CRIMINALS?
WELL, SHE *IS* THE PRINCESS...
WE'RE ALL FIGHTING.
I DON'T KNOW WHERE YOUR PRINCE IS, OR WHAT IT IS THAT THE EVIL WITCHES ARE PLANNING.
BUT WE'RE GOING TO STOP THEM.
OR TRY, AT LEAST.
PRINCESS... DON'T LISTEN TO HER. IT'S ALL JUST NONSENSE.
NICO, BRING THE TEA THAT—
I KNOW WHICH ONE YOU MEAN.

DO YOU WANT TO TRY?
YES. I HAVE TO SAVE WILLIAM.
THEN WE'LL FIGHT TOGETHER!
THIS SMELLS SO GOOD! CAN I...?
GO ON, GO ON! WE PREPARED THE TEA ESPECIALLY FOR YOU.
THAT'S RIGHT, DRINK UP!
PRINCESS, THEY HAVE A FIRE-SPITTING FROG. THEY THREATENED YOU!
I'VE CHANGED MY MIND—AS I SAID BEFORE, I'M STAYING WITH THESE KIND PEOPLE.
NICO, WHAT IS THAT? IT SMELLS FUNNY.
IT WAS ALL A MISUNDERSTANDING.
TELL MY FATHER THAT I'M STAYING WITH MY AUNT. THAT'S AN ORDER!
DON'T WORRY, WE'LL TAKE GOOD CARE OF HER.
THE KING WILL NEVER BELIEVE THAT.
I SAID THAT'S AN ORDER!
BUT PRINCESS...
DID THEY ALL DRINK SOME?
EVERY LAST ONE.
GOOD. THEY WON'T REMEMBER A THING ABOUT THIS PLACE. WELL DONE, NICO.
I HAD A GOOD TEACHER.
I'M SURE I'LL LEARN A LOT FROM YOU, DANI!
OF COURSE!
I'M GLAD THAT YOU'RE STAYING, PRINCESS.
...
LET'S GO. I DON'T TRUST THE FROG KID.
UM... THAT'S MY BROTHER.
...

YAWN.
GOOD MORNING, CARLO!
HUH?
PRINCESS MONICA? SHE'S UP EARLY.
C'MON, DORIAN, THIS IS YOUR CHANCE TO START MAKING SOME FRIENDS.
YOU CAN DO IT!
UH...
GOOD MORNING, PRINCESS—
HUH?
AAAAHHHH!
THUD

WHAT DO YOU THINK YOU'RE DOING, FROG KID?
I COULD ASK YOU THE SAME THING... YOU'RE OUTSIDE MY ROOM.
WHAT? MY ROOM IS UPSTAIRS, IN THE TOWER.
BUT I MIGHT MOVE SO YOU CAN'T CAST A SPELL ON ME WHILE I'M SLEEPING.
I WOULDN'T DO THAT!
I WAS JUST DEFENDING MYSELF YESTERDAY.
I PROPOSE A TRUCE.
FROM NOW ON WE'LL BE CLASSMATES,
SO, BEST TO BE ON GOOD TERMS.
SHOULD I TRUST HIM?
HE THREATENED ME, BUT...
CALL ME DORIAN.
...HE'S JUST A LITTLE KID.
CALL ME MONICA.
OUT OF THE WAY, SLEEPYHEADS!
NICO!

NICO, THAT'S CHEATING!
I DON'T NEED TO CHEAT.
I'M THE BEST AT FLYING!
HA! THERE'S NO WAY YOU CAN BEAT ME.
GOOD MORNING, DANI.
ON THE COUNT OF THREE:
WAIT... YOU SURE THIS ISN'T DANGEROUS?
ONE...
TWO...
THREE!
NICO, YOU JUMPED TOO SOON!
CHEATER!
AH!
HE'S HEADED STRAIGHT DOWN.
LEAVE IT TO ME.

SEE?
NO FAIR!
I'M STILL FASTER THAN YOU.
PHEW! I DON'T KNOW HOW ANYONE ENJOYS RIDING A BROOM.
DON'T TELL ME YOU DON'T KNOW HOW TO RIDE A BROOM...?
HUH?
WHAT KIND OF WITCH ARE YOU?
OF COURSE I KNOW HOW, I JUST DON'T LIKE IT!
AND WHAT KIND OF *PRINCESS* ARE YOU, PRETENDING TO BE A HERO?
WHAT DO YOU MEAN?
DO YOU REALLY THINK YOU CAN SAVE THE PRINCE BY YOURSELF?
YOU COULDN'T DO IT IN YOUR WILDEST DREAMS.
OF COURSE I CAN!
WHY NOT? BECAUSE I'M A GIRL?
BECAUSE YOU'RE A PRINCESS!
WHAT DO YOU KNOW?
DID I GO TOO FAR?
LISTEN, MONICA...

CHAPTER 7

THAT'S PRINCESS MONICA TO YOU!
DON'T SPEAK TO ME EVER AGAIN, FROG KID!
BUT...
TURN
...
GOOD JOB, DORIAN. MESSED UP AGAIN.
HEY, DORIAN!
CAN YOU BRING US A TOWEL?
YEAH, IT'S ALMOST TIME FOR OUR FIRST LESSON.
OKAY, EVERYONE READY? LET'S BEGIN.
MASTER... WHY IS NICO HERE?
I'VE BEEN MASTER'S STUDENT FOR A LOT LONGER THAN YOU.

PLUS, I'M PRINCESS MONICA'S BODYGUARD. SHE PAYS ME VERY WELL.
HE TOLD ME HE KNOWS MARTIAL ARTS!
DON'T LET HIM FOOL YOU.
KIDS, PLEASE, PAY ATTENTION.
TODAY WE'LL TEST EVERYONE'S MAGIC SKILLS.
IT'S COMMON FOR PEOPLE TO HAVE INNATE ABILITIES WHEN IT COMES TO MAGIC.
HUH?
BUT I'M NOT A WITCH.
ANYONE CAN HAVE SOME MAGICAL ABILITY.
DON'T WORRY, YOU CAN'T BE WORSE THAN ME!
BUT I...
...WOULD PREFER NOT TO.
EVERYONE KNOWS WITCHES ARE DEMONS, AND—
...
AH!
I DON'T MEAN TO OFFEND!
DON'T WORRY.
FOR NOW, YOU CAN FOCUS ON LEARNING HOW TO DEFEND YOURSELF.
THE FIRST SPELL IN THE BOOK IS A BASIC OFFENSIVE BATTLE SPELL.
HAVE ANY OF YOU TRIED THIS SPELL?
I HAVE!
LAST YEAR, AT HOME.
I READ ABOUT IT AND, EVEN THOUGH IT'S A PRETTY DIFFICULT SPELL, I MADE OUR NANNY FALL ASLEEP BY ACCIDE—
BOOOOORING!
GOOD FOR YOU, WISE GUY. BUT WE'RE NOT INTERESTED IN YOUR LIFE.
FREAKY...
SHUT UP, NICO!
YOU CAN'T CAST A SINGLE SPELL.
AND WHAT ABOUT YOU, WITCH DANI? YOU'RE A DISASTER.
HEY!
I FORBID YOU FROM MESSING WITH HER!
KIDS, PLEASE...

IT'S SNACK TIME, CARLO!
HERE YOU GO, A FLY...
AND THIS OTHER ONE IS FOR ME, YUM.
...
JUST KIDDING!
ARE YOU HAPPY NOW THAT YOU'RE ALLOWED OUT OF THE BASEMENT? BECAUSE I AM!
YOU'RE THE ONLY ONE WHO UNDERSTANDS ME, CARLO...
MY BEST FRIEND.
YOU'RE GIVING ME THE CREEPS.
AGH! NICO!
WHERE ARE YOU GOING?
MY FRIENDS AND I HEARD ABOUT SOME TALKING BEARS THAT LIVE IN A HOUSE IN THE WOODS.
WE'RE GOING TO CHECK IT OUT.
COOL! CAN I COME?
NO.

C'MON, IT'LL BE FUN! BOYS' DAY OUT.
I HATE TO BREAK IT TO YOU, BUT THERE'S MUD IN THE WOODS.
IT'D BE A SHAME TO GET YOUR FANCY SHOES DIRTY.
THAT'S NOT A PROBLEM!
I'LL ASK THE MASTER TO LEND ME SOME BOOTS.
LISTEN, DUDE.
YOU'RE A FREAK.
I'D BE EMBARRASSED TO INTRODUCE YOU TO MY FRIENDS.
OUTSIDE THIS HOUSE, WE DON'T KNOW EACH OTHER.
GOT IT?
SEE YOU, LOSER!
WAIT, NICO—
DON'T TOUCH ME! I *SAID*, I DON'T LIKE YOU.
HEY!
LEAVE MY BROTHER ALONE!

UGH.
WHERE'S NICO?
HE DISAPPEARED.
DANI, WHAT HAVE YOU DONE?
JUST THE SPELL TO WEAKEN HIM...
THE ONE WE LEARNED THIS MORNING FROM MASTER!
...
HAD YOU TRIED IT BEFORE?
NO...
......
I DON'T THINK I'M CUT OUT TO DO MAGIC.
WHAT AM I GONNA DO NOW, DORIAN?
MAKING PEOPLE DISAPPEAR WITH MAGIC IS EVIL!
HEY! YOU!
STOP CRYING AND PAY ATTENTION!
HUH?
DOWN HERE!
NICO?!
WHAT HAVE YOU DONE TO ME?

OKAY, EVERYONE KEEP CALM.
THERE MUST BE A WAY TO BREAK THE SPELL.
I DON'T KNOW WHY YOU WANT TO HELP HIM, DORIAN. HE DESERVED IT.
YOU'RE SO MEAN!
I THINK HE'S ADORABLE.
BUT I WAS JUST MESSING AROUND!
THE PRINCESS IS RIGHT, NICO.
YOU'RE MUCH CUTER THAN BEFORE.
THAT'S NOT FUNNY.
HERE IT IS!
BOOK OF THE BIG THINGS
A "COUNTER-REDUCING" SPELL.
GET OFF THE TABLE.
OKAY.
REMEMBER, I WAS SIX FEET TALL.
YEAH, SURE! PFFFFFFF!
HA HA HA HA HA HA HA HA HA HA HA HA HA HA HA
WHAT? I WAS!
HERE WE GO.

UH OH.
IT DIDN'T WORK.
YOU CAN'T BE SERIOUS!
HUH... BUT I DID EVERYTHING RIGHT.
MAYBE WE SHOULD ASK THE MASTER.
GREAT IDEA, MONICA!
KARMA.
WHAT DID I TELL YOU? CALL ME PRINCESS...
...FROG KID!
...
HMMM.
CAN YOU FIX HIM, MASTER?
I'VE NEVER HEARD OF SOMEONE USING A WEAKENING SPELL WITH DIFFERENT RESULTS.
YOU CAN'T BE SERIOUS!
BUT I DON'T EVEN KNOW HOW I DID THIS.
YOU'RE THE ONLY ONE THAT CAN FIX IT.
...
I CAN'T LEAVE THE HOUSE LIKE THIS!
YOU DID THIS TO ME, SO YOU'RE RESPONSIBLE.
I GET YOUR ROOM!
NOT IN YOUR WILDEST DREAMS.

FROM NOW ON, YOU'LL SLEEP IN DORIAN'S ROOM.
MINE?
LET ME GO. THIS IS HUMILIATING.
...
...
WELL, NICO, WE CAN HAVE SLEEPOVERS! IT'LL BE FUN.
I'M NOT LIVING WITH THAT GUY.
YES, YOU ARE!
DON'T FIGHT—I'VE HAD A WONDERFUL IDEA.
LOOK AT THIS.
IT'S A MINIATURE COPY OF THE CASTLE.
YOU CAN SLEEP IN MY ROOM!
SLEEPING IN A ROYAL'S ROOM—WHAT A LUXURY.
THAT'S PERFECT, NICO!
THIS IS A NIGHTMARE.
MY ROOM HERE IN THE TOWER IS FINE, BUT I MISS MY SILK CURTAINS AND BOUQUETS OF WHITE ROSES.
I'M GLAD I BROUGHT THIS PIECE OF HOME WITH ME.
I BROUGHT THINGS FROM HOME, TOO!
NOBODY ASKED YOU.

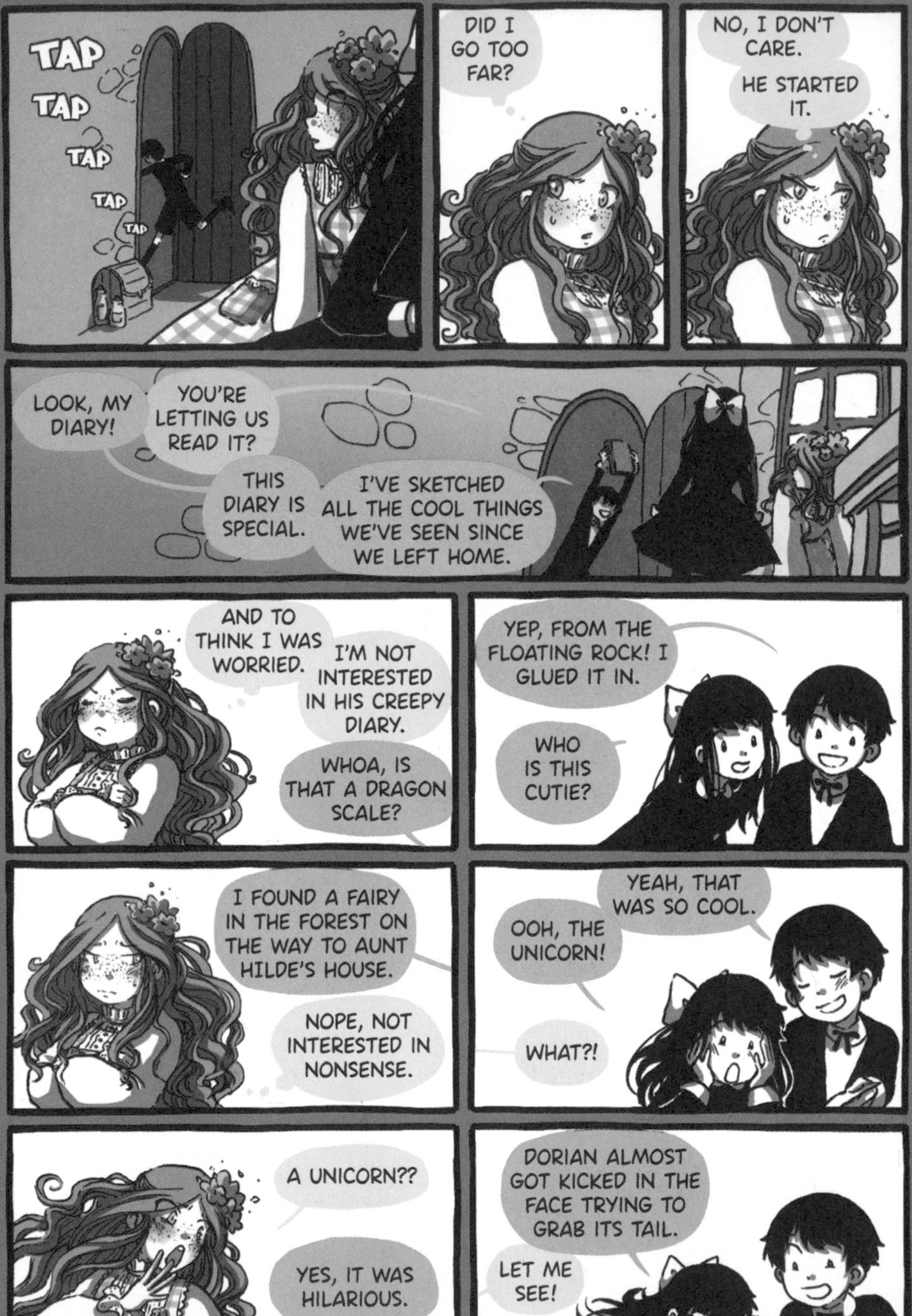
TAP
TAP
TAP
TAP
TAP
DID I GO TOO FAR?
NO, I DON'T CARE.
HE STARTED IT.
LOOK, MY DIARY!
YOU'RE LETTING US READ IT?
THIS DIARY IS SPECIAL.
I'VE SKETCHED ALL THE COOL THINGS WE'VE SEEN SINCE WE LEFT HOME.
AND TO THINK I WAS WORRIED.
I'M NOT INTERESTED IN HIS CREEPY DIARY.
WHOA, IS THAT A DRAGON SCALE?
YEP, FROM THE FLOATING ROCK! I GLUED IT IN.
WHO IS THIS CUTIE?
I FOUND A FAIRY IN THE FOREST ON THE WAY TO AUNT HILDE'S HOUSE.
NOPE, NOT INTERESTED IN NONSENSE.
OOH, THE UNICORN!
YEAH, THAT WAS SO COOL.
WHAT?!
A UNICORN??
YES, IT WAS HILARIOUS.
DORIAN ALMOST GOT KICKED IN THE FACE TRYING TO GRAB ITS TAIL.
LET ME SEE!

OH NOOO!
WHOA, SO CUTE.
MY MONEY FROM THE PRINCESS...
IT SHRANK WITH ME.
I WAS GOING TO BUY A MANSION, AND A MOTORBIKE...
THIS IS ALL YOUR FAULT!
THAT'S WHAT WORRIES YOU? THE MONEY? AREN'T YOU ASHAMED?
WHAT SHOULD I BE WORRIED ABOUT, THEN?
BEING CURSED, FOR EXAMPLE.
AND I'M NOT GOING TO FIGURE IT OUT, EITHER.
NOT UNTIL YOU APOLOGIZE TO DORIAN.
I DON'T WANT TO.
WHY NOT?
NO REASON.
WELL, IF YOU DON'T WANT TO TELL ME, I DON'T CARE.
BUT DON'T BOTHER HIM ANYMORE. OR ELSE.

THIS REMINDED ME OF YOU.
WHAT IS IT? A FAIRY? A MERMAID?
...THAT'S A BIRD.
YES.
A SILLY-LOOKING BIRD.
HUH?
IT LOOKS LIKE CARLO!
REALLY?
WELL...MAYBE IT LOOKS A LITTLE BIT LIKE CARLO...
WHY ARE YOU SAYING I LOOK LIKE A SILLY BIRD?
I DON'T KNOW. IT JUST REMINDED ME OF YOU.
YOU'RE SAYING I'M SILLY, RIGHT?
YE—NO. I MEAN NO.
I DIDN'T MEAN TO SAY THAT!
I DON'T KNOW WHY I BOTHER TALKING TO YOU!
YOU OBVIOUSLY DON'T KNOW HOW TO TALK TO PRINCESSES, LITTLE BROTHER.
HMM...
...BUT DOESN'T IT LOOK LIKE HER?

CHAPTER 8
I HATE SUMMER!
IT'S SO HOOOOT.
BEING THIS TINY DOES HAVE ITS ADVANTAGES.
YOU'RE BEING RIDICULOUS.
RIDICULOUS?
HAVE YOU SEEN YOURSELVES IN THOSE MATCHING OUTFITS?
IS IT REALLY NECESSARY TO MATCH YOUR OUTFITS?
OOOOOH!
I LOVE THE SUSPENDERS!
DAD ALWAYS SAYS THAT A MAN MUST DRESS WITH DISCRETION AND ELEGANCE.
A WISE MAN.
GOOD MORNING, MASTER.
KIDS, I HAVE AN IMPORTANT TASK FOR YOU TODAY.
THERE'S AN EVIL WITCH IN THE FOREST WHO I BEFRIENDED AS A WAY OF SPYING ON HER SCHEMES.
I HAVEN'T HEARD FROM HER IN WEEKS.
NICO, TAKE DANI AND DORIAN TO SEE WHAT'S HAPPENED. MONICA'S TOO RECOGNIZABLE.
IT'S SUCH A CHORE BEING FAMOUS!
HA HA!
KEEP AN EYE ON THEM, NICO.
OF COURSE, MASTER.

GOOD LUCK, DANI!
THANK YOU. WE'LL BE BACK SOON.
... WHAT'S HE WAITING FOR?
DOES HE WANT ME TO SAY GOODBYE TO HIM, TOO?
WELL...
SEE YOU.
FINE...
DORIAN, WAIT.
ER...
WELL...
ABOUT YESTERDAY...
I FORGIVE YOU!
WHAT?

I MEAN...
BUT YOU'RE NOT HELPING WITH ALL YOUR TERRIFYING SPELLS, EITHER.
I'M SORRY I'VE BEEN GRUMPY LATELY.
BUT I KNOW CALLING YOU FROG KID ISN'T RIGHT.
WHY ARE YOU LAUGHING?
PFFT... SORRY.
YOU'RE JUST THE LAST PERSON I'D EVER IMAGINE APOLOGIZING.
THAT'S—
HEY, I'M SORRY, TOO.
WELL THEN...
...WE'RE FRIENDS. OKAY?
...
OKAY.
AS LONG AS FROM NOW ON YOU CALL ME "MR. WYTTE."
...
HA, JUST KIDDING!
SEE YOU LATER, MONICA!
WAIT... WHY DOES WYTTE RING A BELL?

ARE YOU SURE THIS IS THE WAY?
YES, LOOK! THAT'S THE PATH THROUGH THE FOREST.
SINCE WHEN ARE YOU SUCH A GOOD NAVIGATOR?
ARE YOU IMPRESSED, NICO?
I'LL CALL YOU EXPLORER DANI FROM NOW ON.
IT SUITS YOU BETTER THAN QUEEN DANI.
YOU'LL HAVE TO WALK BY YOURSELF IF YOU DON'T WATCH IT.
NO, WAIT!

HMM... I THINK WE'RE CLOSE.
DANI, DON'T BE MEAN! PICK ME UP.
EWW!
WHERE IS ALL THIS MUD COMING FROM?
DORIAN, WE'RE IN THE FOREST! WHAT DID YOU EXPECT?
BUT DO YOU SEE HOW DIRTY MY BOOTS ARE?
SHUT UP. PLEASE.
YOU CAN CLEAN THEM NOW...

WE'VE ARRIVED!
BUT THAT'S...
AWESOOOME!
A WHOLE HOUSE MADE OF CANDY!
AND CHOCOLATE!
I WOULDN'T EAT THAT.
WHY NOT?
CRUNCH
CRUNCH
THIS IS A WITCH'S HOUSE, REMEMBER?
...NEVER MIND.
LOOK, THE DOOR IS OPEN!
WEIRD...
IT SEEMS LIKE THERE'S NO ONE...
IT'S DARK IN HERE.
SO CREEPY.
HEY, LOOK AT THIS!

WHAT DOES IT SAY?
To all witches from all kingdoms, towns, and villages:
You are convened to the first witches' sabbath celebrated after fifteen years of silence.
They chased us, hunted us, and burned us. Now we'll be the hunters.
During the next new moon, we're all
meet in the suspended large rock in
crown our new king. He will guide us
achieve our awaited revenge.
All the activities must be canceled in
pursuit of the common benefit. They, th
schools, and magic tutorships have been
suspended. The kids are with us.
Anyone who doesn't show up will be considered a traitor. We are waiting for you.
THE NEW KING?
THIS SOUNDS BAD...
WE SHOULD BRING THIS LETTER TO THE MASTER.
AGH!
NICO? WHAT'S WRONG?
COME QUICK!
I'LL STAY HERE AND KEEP LOOKING.

THIS IS...
...HORRIBLE.
HUH?
WHAT *IS* THIS??
IT'S AWFUL. THIS...

DID THE WITCH DO THIS?
YES.
SHE'S BEEN EATING CHILDREN, YES.
WHO...?
AND SHE'LL EAT YOU, TOO.
WHOA!
THERE ARE MANY BOOKS AND MANUSCRIPTS!
HUH?
WHAT'S...
...ALL THIS?
I'VE NEVER READ SOMETHING LIKE THIS BEFORE.
THESE SPELLS ARE TERRIFYING.

AHHH!
YOU'RE LUCKY WE FOUND YOU.
I THOUGHT YOU WERE THE WITCH!
HA HA, CALM DOWN!
WE'RE FROM A NEARBY TOWN. WE'RE HERE TO KILL THE WITCH.
BUT WE WERE TOO LATE TO HELP THESE KIDS.
WE SHOULD HAVE BURNED ALL THE WITCHES WHEN WE HAD THE CHANCE.
THE KING IS AN IDIOT FOR THINKING THAT ANY OF THEM CAN BE TRUSTED.
WHAT THIS WOMAN DID IS TERRIBLE... BUT NOT ALL WITCHES ARE BAD.
NO... SHE WOULDN'T...
IF EXPLAINING EVERYTHING WORKED WITH THE PRINCESS...
AFTER ALL...
I'M A WITCH.
STUPID!

UNBELIEVABLE!
WHAT ARE YOU DOING SITTING HERE READING?
HUH?
SOME VILLAGERS KIDNAPPED DANI! THEY'RE GOING TO BURN HER!
HURRY UP, GET YOUR BUTT IN GEAR.
RIGHT!
WHERE DID THEY GO?
TO THE NORTH!
OKAY.
GO TELL THE MASTER WHAT HAPPENED.
WHAT?
CARLO WILL TAKE YOU.

NO WAY!
I WANT TO HELP!
THIS IS THE BEST WAY TO HELP, NICO.
GO AND GET THE MASTER. PLEASE.
...
ARGGH...
OKAY.
BUT DON'T LET THEM SEE YOU DOING ANY SPELLS, OR THEY'LL TRY TO BURN YOU, TOO!
MASTER, HELP! DANI HAS BEEN TAKEN BY SOME VILLAGERS.
DORIAN IS TRYING TO HELP HER, BUT THEY ARE DETERMINED TO BURN HER!
MASTER...
DO YOU HEAR ME?
THEY'RE GOING TO KILL DANI.
MAYBE THAT'S FOR THE BEST.
W-WHAT?

RUN, DORIAN.
I'VE ALWAYS BEEN THE SLOWER TWIN...
C'MON, DORIAN.
WAIT FOR ME!
I ALREADY SEE THE TOWN.
WHERE DO YOU THINK YOU'RE GOING?
WE WERE ALMOST THERE!
YOU KNOW PERFECTLY WELL THAT GOING TO TOWN IS FORBIDDEN.
I'VE TOLD YOU OVER AND OVER THAT YOU AREN'T TO LEAVE THE HOUSE.
I'M SORRY, DAD...
IT'S NOT FAIR!
IF I SAY "NO," IT MEANS "NO"! DON'T YOU SEE IT'S DANGEROUS?

NOTHING HAPPENED. THERE'S NO NEED TO SCARE THEM, HANS.
MOMMYYYY! HI!
YOU'RE NOT GOING TO LEAVE AGAIN, ARE YOU?
YOU CAN'T PLAY WITH THE OTHER KIDS.
IF THEY NOTICE THAT YOU'RE WITCHES, WE'LL ALL BE IN TROUBLE.
NO!
PROMISE!
IT'S NOT ALL RIGHT.
ALL RIGHT, NOW HUG YOUR GRUMPY FATHER.
DAD GETS MAD ABOUT EVERYTHING.
DAD JUST WANTS YOU TO BE SAFE. OUTSIDE THERE ARE PEOPLE WHO CAN HURT YOU.
WHEN WE GROW UP, WE'LL BE FRIENDS WITH EVERYONE!
DAD ALREADY HAS PLANS FOR YOU.
WHEN YOU GROW UP, OTHER PEOPLE WON'T BE A PROBLEM ANYMORE.
WE'LL HAVE TAKEN OUR REVENGE.

AT THE TIME, I DIDN'T UNDERSTAND WHAT MY MOTHER MEANT...
WE'VE CAUGHT THE WITCH FROM THE WOODS!
SHE'S THE ONE THAT'S BEEN KIDNAPPING OUR KIDS.
SHE KILLED THEM!
WE FOUND THIS BOOK FILLED WITH EVIL SPELLS.
BURNING WITCHES HAS BEEN OUTLAWED, BUT WE SAY THIS IS A SPECIAL CASE.
WHAT DO YOU SAY?
YES!
SHE DESERVES IT.
KILL HER!
JUSTICE!
BURN HER.
BUT NOW I THINK OUR DAD WAS RIGHT.
DORIAN...

...WHERE ARE YOU?
HOW LONG HAVE I BEEN RUNNING?
I CAN'T DO THIS ANYM—
AGH!
POW!
UGH...
I'M COMING FOR YOU, DANI!

CHAPTER 9

THAT WAY.
WHY DID THIS GUY HAVE TO COME TOO?
WHAT IF HE NOTICES ME?
WE HAD NO CHOICE.
HERE WE GO.
WE'LL BE THERE IN HALF AN HOUR!
HE'S THE ONLY PERSON I KNOW WITH A CAR.
WHAT I REALLY WONDER IS
WHAT'S ACTUALLY GOING ON IN MASTER'S HEAD?
I KNOW YOU DON'T UNDERSTAND, BUT...
MAYBE THAT'S FOR THE BEST.
W-WHAT?
HOW COULD YOU SAY THAT?
MASTER...
WHY?

DO YOU REALLY WANT TO LET HER—
WHAT'S GOING ON HERE?!
WHAT ARE YOU DOING?
WHERE ARE DANI AND DORIAN?
...
WHY ARE BOTH OF YOU SO SERIOUS?
HEY! ARE YOU LISTENING TO ME?
NICO!
AH!
YES!
SOME GUYS KIDNAPPED DANI AND THEY PLAN TO BURN HER BECAUSE THEY FOUND OUT SHE'S A WITCH!
WHAT?!
WHY ARE YOU JUST STANDING THERE?!
HURRY!
WE MUST SAVE HER!
WAIT!
HURRY, NICO!
THERE'S NO TIME TO WASTE.
BUT WHAT ARE YOU GONNA DO?
I'M THE PRINCESS!
I HAVE MY OWN RESOURCES.

I'M ALMOST THERE!
BURN THAT WITCH!
YOU'RE A MONSTER.
DIE!
I GUESS WE ALL AGREE!
YES!
OF COURSE.
DO IT!
OH NO...
OKAY, THEN. SHE MUST BURN.
DANI!
NO...
I...

I HAVE TO...
DO...
SOMETHING!!
I MUST.
HURRY, DORIAN... YOUR WAND.
THIS IS OUR MOMENT!
OUR REVENGE!
WHERE IS IT?
IT SHOULD BE HERE!
I CAN'T BELIEVE IT.
WHERE IS IT?
HURRY...
AAAAAARGH
IN THE MEMORY OF OUR CHILDREN.

DANI!
OH NO!
LET ME PAST!
UGH.
PLEASE!
AAH.
DANI!

AAH!
I'M INNOCENT!
NO, PLEASE!
AAAAH!
PLEASE!

SPLASH!
WHAT THE—
BOOOO!
BURN HER!
WHAT WAS THAT?
WHO EXTINGUISHED THE FIRE?
ME.
HUFF
HUFF
ARE YOU OUT OF YOUR MIND?!
THIS IS INHUMAN.
WHO DO YOU THINK YOU ARE, BRAT?
ISN'T SHE...?

STAND ASIDE.
POW!
WITCH-HUNTING IS FORBIDDEN.
IS THAT SO?
YES.
WHO'S GOING TO STOP ME?
OH!
IT CAN'T BE...!
MAYBE YOU SHOULD BURN, TOO!
WAIT—
DON'T YOU DARE TOUCH ME!
DON'T YOU KNOW WHO I AM?
POW!
WHAT THE HELL ARE YOU DOING?!
WHAT ARE *YOU* DOING?
TRYING TO BURN LITTLE GIRLS?
YOU'RE GONNA PAY FOR THIS!
IDIOT.
ER—HOLD ON...
POW
POW

SHE'S THE PRINCESS, RIGHT?
OH NO!
THEY'RE IN TROUBLE...
WHAT SHOULD WE DO?
I BETTER GET GOING.
AH...
WHAT A RELIEF.
SHE'S OKAY.
WHY DIDN'T YOU HELP THEM, MASTER?
I'VE ALREADY DONE TOO MUCH BY DRIVING YOU HERE.
I TOLD YOU BEFORE.
I'M NOT SURE WE'RE DOING THE RIGHT THING.
I DON'T GET IT.
WHY ARE YOU SAYING THAT?
MASTER... TELL ME.
YOU'LL FIND OUT SOON,
WHEN THE RIGHT MOMENT ARRIVES.
WHATEVER. I'M GOING TO HELP DANI.
DON'T LET THEM SEE YOU.
AND NICO, JUST ONE LAST THING...
SURE...
DON'T GET TOO ATTACHED TO THEM.
LATER!

DANI?
OPEN YOUR EYES.
HERE...
BE CAREFUL.
ARE YOU OKAY?
DANI!
ANSWER ME, PLEASE!
DANI!
ARE YOU ALL RIGHT?!
CAN YOU STAND BY YOURSELF?
DANI...
NOD
UM...
ARE YOU SURE?
UH...

WAAAAAH!
OH.
WAAAAH!
...
OH, DANI.
COME HERE.
SNIFF...
SNIFF...
AH...
HUH?
UM...
COME ON NOW.
THERE, THERE.

WAAAAH!
DANI!
DANI...

HEY, DORIAN...
...DID YOU NOTICE HOW BRAVE I WAS? I SAVED DANI!
SURE.
OF COURSE, IT WAS YOUR FATHER WHO ORDERED THE BURNING OF WITCHES IN THE FIRST PLACE.
THAT WAS SO LONG AGO! IT'S NOT EVEN LEGAL ANYMORE.
BESIDES, I WOULD NEVER BURN ANYONE.
DORIAN!
YOU TRIED THE DAY YOU MET US.
BLAM!
HE'S SO MAD...
YOU DON'T THINK I'M A BAD PERSON, RIGHT?

"THEY CHASED US, HUNTED US, AND BURNED US."
"NOW WE'LL BE THE HUNTERS."
...
DORIAN?
DANI?
WHAT ARE YOU DOING HERE?
I CAN'T SLEEP...
CAN I STAY WITH YOU TONIGHT?
OF COURSE YOU CAN.
I'M SO SORRY, DORIAN.
I SHOULDN'T HAVE SAID I WAS A WITCH.
IT WASN'T YOUR FAULT.
BUT WE SHOULD DO SOMETHING ABOUT IT.
WHAT ARE YOU TALKING ABOUT?
I WAS READING THE LETTER WE FOUND AT THE WITCH'S HOUSE.
I THINK WE SHOULD GO TO THE SABBATH.
I KNOW MONICA'S FATHER IS ALREADY KING. AND THAT WE ALWAYS WANTED TO LEAVE HOME AND MAKE FRIENDS.
BUT IN THE END, WE'RE STILL WITCHES.

CHAPTER 10

MAKING POTIONS IS THE SAFEST WAY TO PRACTICE MAGIC WITHOUT RAISING SUSPICION.
UGH.
IT'S THE OLDEST DISCIPLINE IN THE MAGIC COMMUNITY...
HOW DEPRESSING.
...AND IT CAN...
BLAH BLAH BLAH...
THIS IS UNBEARABLE.
I HAVE TO DO SOMETHING.

AHA! I'VE GOT IT!
LET'S GO TO THE BEACH!
WHAT? TO THE BEACH?
BUT THE POTION EXAM—
WE COULD MAKE A POTION FROM MARINE INGREDIENTS.
COME ON, IT WILL BE FUN!
YES!
THIS CLASS IS A TOTAL BORE.
COME ON, DANI.
WE CAN BUILD SANDCASTLES AND GO SNORKELING!
BEEEEACH DAAAAYY!
DORIAN, YOU'RE NOT GOING?
I DON'T FEEL LIKE IT.
WHAT ABOUT THE EXAM? YOU CAN'T MISS IT.
...

WHAT A BEAUTIFUL DAY.
NO CLOUDS IN THE SKY!
COME ON, DANI, LET'S RACE.
I TOLD YOU, I CAN'T SWIM!
YOU'RE SCARED OF LOSING, HUH? EVEN THOUGH I'M TINY?
ME, SCARED?!
WAIT, DANI—
SPLASH!

WHAT ARE YOU DOING?
YOU HAVEN'T PUT ON SUNSCREEN!
...
WHAT?
YOU'LL GET SUNBURNED IF YOU'RE NOT CAREFUL.
SPLASH
AAAAGH!
DORIAN!
QUICK, DANI, TELL YOUR BROTHER TO PUT SOME SUNSCREEN ON, TOO!
TELL HIM YOURSELF.
I CAN'T! HE'S SO MAD AT ME.
PLEASE, DANI...
...
DO IT FOR DORIAN!
OKAY...
SO... COLD...
HEY, DORIAN!
MONICA SAYS YOU HAVE TO PUT ON SOME SUNSCREEN.
I CAN TAKE CARE OF MYSELF.
HE'S REALLY MAD AT YOU, HUH?
I KNEW IT. HE HATES ME!

ARE YOU MAD AT *HIM*? MAKE UP YOUR MIND!
I DON'T KNOW!
STOP CHITCHATTING AND LET'S GO SWIMMING.
I'M GOING TO LOOK AT THE BOOKS THAT MASTER PENDRAGON GAVE US.
OKAY, DANI, WATCH AND LEARN.
HOW CAN SHE BE SO CAREFREE?
I DON'T GET IT...
LET THE EXPERT SHOW YOU—
...
AAAAAH, HEEEEELP!
SHARK!
HA HA HA HA HA!
IT'S JUST A LITTLE FISH!
HA HA HA HA
STOP LAUGHING!
YOU'RE PRETTY FAST FOR BEING SO LITTLE!

HEY, DANI...
I'M SO GLAD YOU'RE FEELING BETTER.
I WAS AFRAID THAT AFTER WHAT HAPPENED YOU'D STOP TRUSTING...
AH...
YOU KNOW.
US.
I WOULD HAVE NEVER IMAGINED THAT SOMETHING LIKE THAT WOULD HAPPEN.
MY PARENTS WARNED ME, BUT I DIDN'T THINK PEOPLE STILL HATED WITCHES SO MUCH.
BUT THERE'S NO WAY I'D STOP TRUSTING YOU, NICO.
YOU SAVED ME!
THANK YOU SO MUCH.
WHAT ARE YOU TALKING ABOUT?
I COULDN'T DO ANYTHING.
IF IT HADN'T BEEN FOR YOU...MASTER, MONICA, AND MARK WOULD HAVE BEEN TOO LATE.
AND YOU COULD HAVE PROBABLY BEATEN ALL THOSE GUYS IF I HADN'T...
...AHEM...
...SHRUNK YOU.
SORRY—
YOU CAN SAY THAT AGAIN!
I MIGHT HAVE NO IDEA HOW TO DO MAGIC...
...BUT I WILL ALWAYS BE ON THE WITCHES' SIDE.
ON *YOUR* SIDE!

THANK GOODNESS!
I THOUGHT YOU WERE MAD AT ME, TOO, DANI.
OF COURSE NOT.
NOW, HOW WILL YOU THANK THE MUFFIN GUY?
HE WAS SO KIND, LENDING US HIS VAN.
MARK?
I DON'T KNOW, MAYBE I SHOULD THANK HIM...
BUT I CRIED LIKE A BABY.
WHAT MUST HE THINK OF ME?
WAIT... IS IT POSSIBLE?
DO YOU *LIKE* HIM?!
COME ON, DON'T BE STUPID.
I DO.
A BIT.
WHAT?!
HEHE!
I KNEW IT!
YOU CAN'T BE SERIOUS!
HE'S SO HANDSOME.
HE'S AN IDIOT!
HE LOOKS LIKE A PRINCE.
I MEAN, HE'S NOT BAD, BUT HE'S NO PRINCE.
BUT HE'S SO HANDSOME. AND BRAVE!

BUT A PRINCE IS ALSO KIND, POLITE, CULTURED, CHIVALROUS, ELEGANT...
HE MUST SPEAK AND DRESS PERFECTLY, AND RESCUE DAMSELS.
AHEM.
LIKE MY WILL!
OOOH, I SEE!
DORIAN, HAVE YOU CAUGHT A COLD? IN THIS HOT WEATHER?
WE COULD MAKE A COUGH POTION.
...
NO, I DON'T HAVE A COLD.
I'VE JUST HAD A WONDERFUL IDEA.
HERE IT IS!
WE CAN MAKE A LOVE POTION FOR MARK.
E LOVE POTION
WHAT?!
NO WAY!
THAT'S A HORRIBLE IDEA.
HE'S OUR ARCHENEMY, DANI!

HE'S NICER THAN YOU!
SHUT UP!
GUYS, DON'T FIGHT.
NICO, YOU MUST SUPPORT TRUE LOVE!
WHA— LOVE?!
L... LOVE...?!
OKAY! ENOUGH!
I'M DONE WITH THIS.
COME ON, DORIAN!
OKAY, BYE.
LET'S IGNORE THESE STUPID GIRLS, MY FRIEND.
FRIEND?
...
LET'S GO, DANI— IT'S GOING TO BE A GREAT DAY.
WE'LL WEAR OUR NEW SUITS, PASS THE EXAM, AND CONQUER LOVE!
ARE... ARE YOU SURE...?

AHA! I FOUND IT!
AND I'VE GOT THE PINK CORAL.
A FEW DROPS OF THIS...
...AND THE FINAL INGREDIENT...
HOW EXCITING!
BOOM!
IT LOOKS LIKE THEY'RE HAVING FUN.
...

DO YOU PLAN TO STICK YOUR NOSE IN THAT BOOK FOR A LONG TIME?
I HAVE TO LOCATE THE APPROPRIATE INGREDIENTS.
BUT DON'T WORRY.
AS SOON AS I'M DONE, WE'LL GO PLAY IN THE WAVES.
WE'LL HAVE A BLAST. YOU'LL SEE.
...
DON'T GET TOO EXCITED. I'M JUST HERE BECAUSE...
BECAUSE I ARGUED WITH YOUR SISTER.
AH...
BESIDES, HOW LONG DOES IT TAKE TO CHECK A LIST OF INGREDIENTS?
WELL... ACTUALLY...
I CAN'T SWIM.
?
HA HA HA
SHH!
ARE YOU SERIOUS?!
ASK THE PRINCESS FOR A FLOATY, LIKE DANI.
NO WAY!
DUDE, WHY ARE YOU SO MAD AT HER?
I'M NOT MAD AT HER. BUT...
BUT WHAT?
I KNOW THAT WHAT HAPPENED WASN'T HER FAULT, BUT SHE'S STILL THE PRINCESS.
I FEEL LIKE I'M BETRAYING THE WITCHES WHEN I SPEAK TO HER.
I DON'T KNOW WHAT TO DO.

YOU'RE FREAKING ME OUT.
WHAT HAPPENED WAS TERRIBLE.
BUT I DON'T BLAME YOU OR DANI FOR THAT WITCH WHO WAS EATING KIDS
AND YOU SHOULDN'T BLAME ALL OF US NON-MAGICAL PEOPLE, EITHER.
...
NOW DROP THAT BOOK ONCE AND FOR ALL.
I'M GONNA TEACH YOU HOW TO SWIM!
AT LEAST I'LL TRY.
IS THIS THE RIGHT WAY?
YES, IT SHOULDN'T BE TOO FAR AWAY...
CAN'T YOU LET GO OF THAT ROCK?
YOUR FEET TOUCH THE GROUND HERE.
ARE YOU SURE?
YES!
BY THE WAY, WHAT ARE WE LOOKING FOR EXACTLY?
OH, JUST...

A GIANT SQUID!
OUR LOVE POTION...
...IS FINISHED.
AAAAGH!
DORIAN...?
HELP!
DORIAN!
WHAT HAPPENED?!
YOUR STUPID BROTHER WENT LOOKING FOR IT, FOR THE POTION EXAM!
I LOST MY WAND...
BUT I'VE GOT THIS!

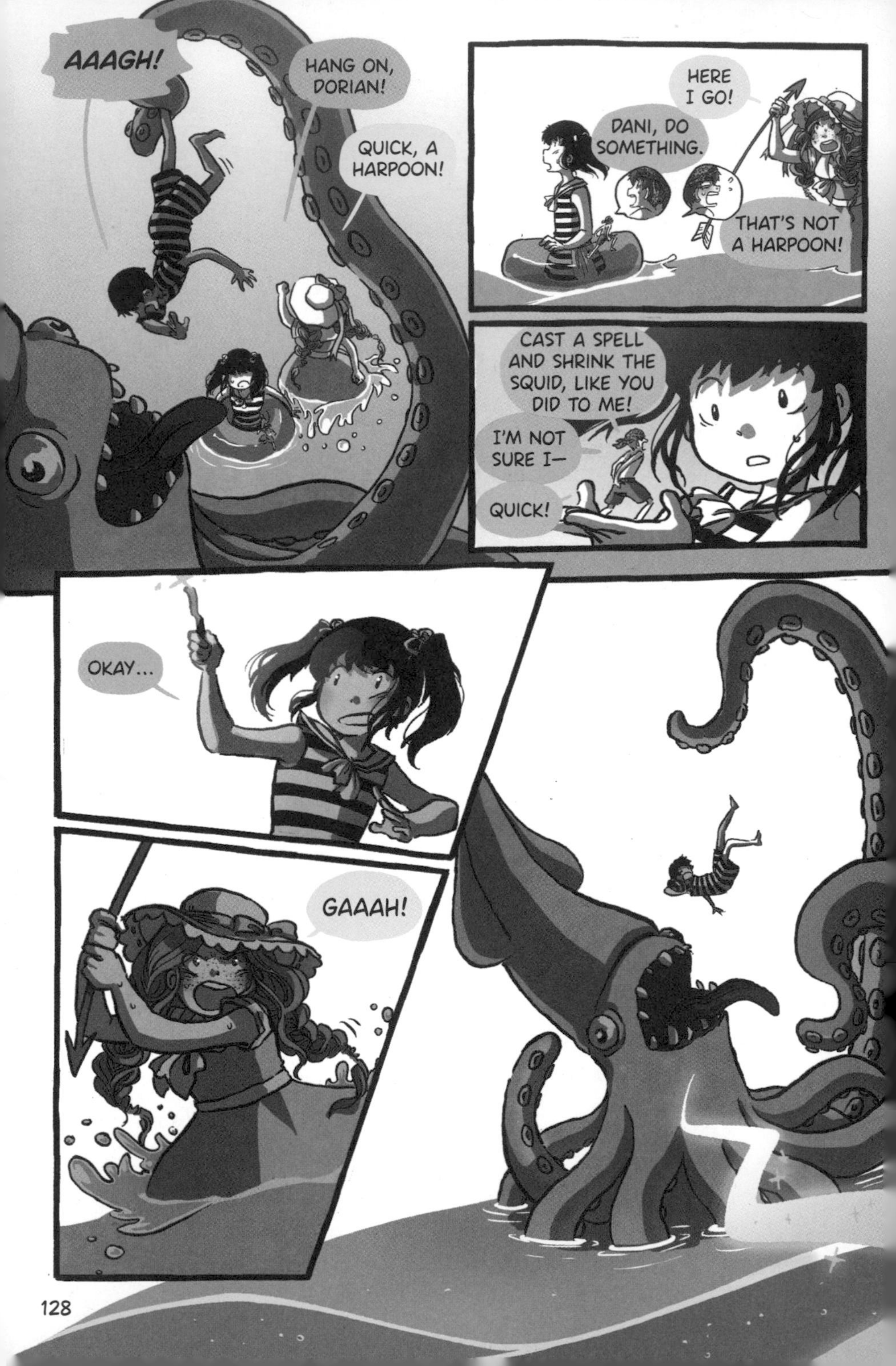
AAAGH!
HANG ON, DORIAN!
QUICK, A HARPOON!
HERE I GO!
DANI, DO SOMETHING.
THAT'S NOT A HARPOON!
CAST A SPELL AND SHRINK THE SQUID, LIKE YOU DID TO ME!
I'M NOT SURE I—
QUICK!
OKAY...
GAAAH!

DORIAN...?
WHERE IS HE?
UGH...
MISSION ACCOMPLISHED!
WHO GOES SEARCHING FOR A GIANT SQUID? DO YOU WANNA DIE?!
DANI... WHICH SPELL DID YOU CAST?
THE SAME ONE I USED ON NICO. WHY?
WELL, I THINK THE SQUID...
...IS DEAD.

CREEPY...
I DIDN'T MEAN TO...
DON'T WORRY, DANI.
YOU SAVED MY LIFE, AND THAT'S WHAT COUNTS!
OKAY, DORIAN...
THIS IS THE MOMENT.
HEY, MONICA—
LET'S FOCUS ON WHAT'S IMPORTANT: DANI AND MUFFIN GUY!
ENOUGH! LET'S GO, DORIAN.
YOU MIGHT EVEN GET A KISS! CAN YOU IMAGINE?
HUH?!
WAIT, I DON'T KNOW ABOUT ALL THAT!
TRUST ME.
I'M AN EXPERT ON LOVE.
OKAY, OKAY. LET'S ORDER SOME BAKED GOODS, DANI.
OKAY.

WHAT POTION DID YOU WANT GIANT SQUID INK FOR, ANYWAY?
I'M GOING TO MAKE A POTION TO GET YOU BACK TO YOUR REAL SIZE.
ARE YOU SERIOUS?!
DORIAN, YOU'RE THE BEST!
I KNOW, I KNOW.
YOU'RE NOT AS USELESS AS YOU LOOK!
THANK... YOU?
I HOPE IT WORKS.
WHY...
...DIDN'T IT WORK?!
I DON'T KNOW...
I DRANK ALL THIS GROSS POTION FOR NOTHING!
YOU'RE USELESS!
BUT—
HOW CAN YOU PLAY WITH PEOPLE'S FEELINGS LIKE THAT?
HEY, NICO, WAIT!
I CAN TRY AGAI—
NO WAY!!

I CAN'T STAY, I'M WORKING.
C'MON, STAY WITH US FOR A PICNIC.
THERE ARE TOO MANY MUFFINS FOR THE TWO OF US.
BUT YOU ORDERED THEM.
HEY, MARK!
COME ON!
...
OKAY.
BUT I'M STAYING JUST FOR TEN MINUTES.
YAY!
GO AHEAD TO THE BEACH, I'LL GO GET...
...AH... SOMETHING!
OKAY...
I HAVE TO GIVE THIS TO HIM?
I'M NOT SURE I CAN...
HOW ARE YOU?
HUH?
YOU KNOW, AFTER THE OTHER DAY...
I'M FINE!
WELL, I BROUGHT THIS TO CHEER YOU UP.
RAISIN BREAD PUDDING AGAIN?
EW...
GREAT...
NEXT TIME JUST DON'T GO AROUND
TELLING STRANGERS YOU'RE A WITCH.

WHAT?! DID YOU ALREADY KNOW I WAS A WITCH?!
?
OF COURSE.
IT'S NOT LIKE YOU TRY TO HIDE IT.
BESIDES, YOU LIVE WITH MASTER PENDRAGON.
AND NICO MENTIONED SOMETHING...
HEY.
I JUST RAN AWAY FROM HOME.
THE MASTER IS AN IDIOT!
HUH?
I'M STAYING HERE.
OH NO...
IT WAS OBVIOUS?
I DIDN'T MEAN TO FRIGHTEN YOU.
IT'S OBVIOUS BECAUSE I PAY ATTENTION!
BESIDES, YOU'RE SAFE IN THIS TOWN.
WE DON'T KILL PEOPLE FOR WITCHCRAFT AROUND HERE.
PENDRAGON HAS ALWAYS HELPED US WITH HIS MAGIC.
AND, ER...
...YOU CAN TRUST ME. EVEN IF YOU DON'T BELIEVE IT.
WHAT DO YOU MEAN?

WELL, YOU HID THE FACT THAT YOU'RE A WITCH.
BUT I GET IT. I HAVE NOTHING TO DO WITH MAGIC.
OH. REALLY?
MARK, YOU'RE WRONG. I WANT US TO BE FRIENDS.
ACTUALLY, I WOULD REALLY LIKE US TO BE FRIENDS.
GROSS.
WHO DOES HE THINK HE IS?
I FEEL TERRIBLE.
MAYBE I SHOULD ABORT "MISSION LOVE POTION"...
THEN THE HOUSE STARTED BURNING!

AND WE HAD TO CLEAN AGAIN.
SO, YOU'RE HOPELESS WITH MAGIC.
WHAT?
DON'T MAKE FUN OF ME!
IT'S OKAY, I WAS A DISASTER AT SCHOOL TOO!
WHOA, I'M THIRSTY. CAN I HAVE THIS?
HUH?!
OH NO! HE'S DRINKING THE POTION!
THIS CAN'T BE HAPPENING.
HEY, THIS TASTES KINDA WEIRD.
HUH?
HEY, DANI... I JUST REALIZED SOMETHING.
ABOUT YOU.
WHAT?
DANI, I...
HEY, WHAT ARE YOU DOING?
MARK, WAIT... THERE'S BEEN A MISTAKE—
NO... I REALLY...
I REALLY HATE YOU.
YOU MUST DIE.

I'M NOT SURE IF THIS IS A GOOD IDEA.
THE ROOM IS FINE, BUT BORING.
I REALLY LOVE WHITE ROSES! BUT THERE AREN'T ANY AROUND HERE.
I TOOK THE ROSE WITHOUT THINKING...
...BUT NOW'S NOT THE TIME TO CHANGE MY MIND!
I HAVE TO APOLOGIZE.
COME ON, DORIAN. YOU CAN DO IT!
...
I CAN'T!!
I WAS TOO MEAN. THERE'S NO WAY SHE'LL FORGIVE ME THAT EASILY.
STUPID FROG KID!
WHAT WOULD PRINCE WILLIAM DO?

PLEASE, ACCEPT THIS PRESENT AS AN APOLOGY, LOVELY YOUNG LADY.
MAY I HAVE THE HONOR OF THIS DANCE?
DON'T BE AFRAID, PRINCESS!
THAT'S WHAT PRINCES DO.
THERE THEY ARE! HOW ROMANTIC.
THIS IS BETTER THAN A ROMANCE NOVEL.
KNOCK
KNOCK
AH! HI, DORIAN.
HELLO.
I WAS JUST SEEING HOW DANI'S DATE IS GOING.
DO YOU WANT TO TAKE A LOOK?
UH... NO, THANKS.
THE THING IS...
ACCEPT THIS PRESENT AS AN APOLOGY.
PLEASE.
YOU SAID THAT YOU LIKE THEM, AND—
OOOOOH.
A WHITE ROSE! THANK YOU.
AAAAAH!

SOUNDS LIKE SOMETHING HAPPENED...
OKAY. SEE YA.
LET'S SEE HOW EVERYTHING IS GOING BETWEEN THE LOVEBIRDS!
BLAM
THEY'RE GONE!
WHERE DID THEY GO?
THAT'S WHAT HAPPENS WHEN I GET DISTRACTED...
AH...
WHAT WAS THAT?!
MARK JUST TRIED TO KILL ME!
PHEW. I THINK I LOST HIM.
DANI!
NICO?

WHAT HAPPENED?!
I THINK IT WAS MY POTION...
BUT WE FOLLOWED ALL THE INSTRUCTIONS.
I DON'T KNOW.
THEN HOW—
EVERY TIME I TRY TO DO MAGIC, I MAKE A MESS.
I'M SO TIRED OF IT.
QUICK, CAST A SPELL ON HIM!
I CAN'T!
DANI...
I KNOW YOU'RE THERE.
DON'T RUN AWAY.
MARK, STOP IT!
LET HER...
AAAH!
...GO.

CHAPTER 11

I SAID STOP!
!
AAARGH!
POW!
WHAT... NICO?
DUDE, I'M BLEEDING!
SO-SORRY...
BUT WHY DID YOU GET IN MY WAY?
WHY?! YOU WERE GOING TO HIT DANI!
DANI...
WAIT!
NO, NO, NO—
PUNCH!
AAAAAH!
WHAT HAPPENED?
MY POTION DIDN'T WORK AS PLANNED.
BUT YOURS DID! I'M NORMAL AGAIN.
YES, BUT WHY DO YOU HAVE A HALF-DEAD GUY WITH YOU?
CAN HE SLEEP HERE TONIGHT?

THE POTION MUST HAVE MADE HIM SICK.
I KNOCKED HIM OUT!
YOU WERE LUCKY HE HIT HIS HEAD.
IS HE DEAD?!
DIDN'T YOU HAVE TO SAY SOMETHING TO DORIAN?
REALLY?
NICO...
FINE.
THANK YOU SO MUCH FOR MY POTION, DORIAN!
HUH?
YOU'RE NOT SO BAD AFTER ALL.
IT WAS NOTHING. I'M GLAD YOU RECOGNIZE MY WORTH.
ALL RIGHT... I'M OUT OF HERE!
GOOD NIGHT.
WHERE ARE YOU GONNA SLEEP?
I'LL MANAGE ON MY OWN.
STAYING IN THE SAME ROOM AS MY ARCHENEMY AND THAT NERD DORIAN?
NO WAY.
HEY, NICO. THANKS FOR HELPING ME TODAY.
DORIAN...
WHAT'S THE MATTER?
I'M FINE.
COME ON, YOU CAN TELL ME.
IT'S JUST...
WELL...
I HAVE NO FRIENDS.
THAT'S IT? YOU SCARED ME!
WHAT DO YOU MEAN, "THAT'S IT"?
SORRY.
FOR A MOMENT, I THOUGHT YOU WANTED TO GO TO THE SABBATH AND TAKE REVENGE!
CRAZY, RIGHT?

Y-YES, CRAZY...
AS YOUR OLDER SISTER, HERE'S SOME ADVICE...
JUST BE YOURSELF!
THANKS A LOT! AND YOU'RE ONLY OLDER BY A FEW MINUTES. DOESN'T COUNT.
AT HOME, EVERYONE LIKED YOU.
WHO? MOM AND DAD? THE GARDENER, THE COOK? THEY'RE ADULTS.
I FEEL LIKE I DON'T FIT IN ANYWHERE.
HOW DO YOU DO IT, DANI? EVERYONE LIKES YOU.
DORIAN, YOU'RE OVERTHINKING IT. NICO AND MONICA REALLY LIKE YOU, I'M SURE.
IN FACT, THEY WERE WORRIED ABOUT YOU TODAY.
YOU SHOULDN'T WORRY ABOUT SILLY THINGS.
WELL, YOU WORRY ABOUT SILLY THINGS TOO.
I DO?
I DON'T UNDERSTAND WHAT'S SO FUN ABOUT ROMANCE.
A WAR IS COMING, AND YOU'RE THINKING ABOUT LOVE.
STOP IT, *DAD!* I'M GOING TO BED.
WAIT, DANI.
ARE *YOU* ALL RIGHT?
HUH...? I'M FINE.
PERFECTLY FINE.
YOU SURE?
YES, DEFINITELY!!
DON'T YOU WORRY.
OKAY...
GOOD NIGHT.
NIGHT, DORIAN.

CHAPTER 12

WHAT TIME IS IT?
MY DAD IS GONNA KILL M—
AGH!
GOOD MORNING.
THE POTION DIDN'T WORK?
NO... ACTUALLY, HE TRIED TO KILL ME.
WHAT?!
BUT WE FOLLOWED THE RECIPE EXACTLY!
I KNOW...
MASTER! WHAT SHOULD WE DO?
I'VE NEVER HEARD OF A LOVE POTION CAUSING THAT REACTION.
WHERE'S THE BOY?
IN DORIAN'S ROOM.
DORIAN'S ROOM?!
ISN'T THAT DANGEROUS? YOU TWO LOOK ALIKE!
...
NOW THAT YOU MENTION IT...
WHOA, IT SOUNDS GREAT!
YEAH, I WENT LAST YEAR AND IT WAS AMAZING.

YOU SHOULD GO. BUT BE CAREFUL, IT CAN BE DANGEROUS.
THERE'S NO DANGER THAT CAN STOP ME!
HAHA. I SEE THAT.
GOOD MORNING!
I'M GLAD YOU'RE FEELING BETTER, MARK.
YES, MUCH... BETTER...
PUT THAT KNIFE DOWN.
TIME TO GO!
LET'S HANG OUT SOMETIME.
HUH?
WHERE AM I?
REALLY...? "GUY STUFF"?
NEXT TIME LET'S DO GUY STUFF!
SURE, WHENEVER.
WHAT?!
SEE YOU!
BYE!
BYE, CARLO!
I MADE MY FIRST FRIEND!
FIRST?!
MARK IS SO NICE!
I TOLD YOU, HE'S AN ENEMY!
NICO?
WHAT HAPPENED?! WHY ARE YOU SMALL AGAIN?

FINALLY, SOMEONE NOTICED.
DID YOU USE GIANT SQUID'S INK?
YES, AMONG OTHER THINGS...
SQUID INK WAS A GOOD IDEA.
BUT MARINE POTIONS ARE AFFECTED BY THE MOON, JUST LIKE TIDES.
AT THE FULL MOON AND NEW MOON, THEY ARE MUCH MORE POWERFUL.
WHAT?!
BUT IT SHOULD STILL HAVE SOME EFFECT AT OTHER TIMES.
WHICH PROVES HOW POWERFUL DANI'S SPELL IS.
SHE'S STILL THE ONLY ONE THAT CAN UNDO IT.
YES!
WELL DONE, DORIAN!
MASTER... DO YOU HAVE A BETTER WAND TO LEND ME?
NO.
MASTER, HOW DO YOU UNDO THIS SPELL?
TAKE A LOOK... PAGE 52.
I WANT TO SEE TOO!
MASTER, I HAVE A QUESTION.
NEXT WEEK THERE'S A METEOR SHOWER.
MY SISTER AND I WANT TO GO WATCH IT.
CAN WE SKIP A COUPLE OF DAYS?
NO. WE'VE LOST TOO MUCH TIME ALREADY.
YOU HAVE MANY THINGS TO LEARN AND WE DON'T KNOW HOW LONG WE'LL BE SAFE.
BUT IT'S JUST FOR A COUPLE OF DAYS—
THERE'S NOTHING TO DISCUSS.

DORIAN, WAIT! WHY DIDN'T YOU TELL ME ABOUT THE METEOR SHOWER BEFORE?
MARK MENTIONED IT THIS MORNING.
HE MENTIONED A SPECIFIC PLACE IN THE WOODS WHERE YOU CAN SEE IT PERFECTLY.
ARE WE GOING WITH HIM?!
UNLESS YOU WANT TO DIE, NO.
WE'LL GO ALONE.
IT'S NEXT TO THE FLOATING ROCK, WHERE THE WITCH'S PRISON IS.
AND IT'S THE SAME NIGHT AS THE WITCHES' SABBATH.
WHAT...?
DORIAN...
I DON'T THINK WE SHOULD GO.
WHAT WOULD DAD AND MOM SAY?
AND WHAT DO YOU WANT TO DO?
JUST STAY HERE AND DO NOTHING?!
IT'S NOT LIKE WE CAN CHANGE ANYTHING.
I WANT TO KNOW WHAT'S GOING ON, AND WHY.
I WANT TO DO SOMETHING. I DON'T CARE WHAT THE MASTER SAYS.
WE'RE GOING.
YOU AND I WILL LEAVE THE NIGHT BEFORE THE METEOR SHOWER...
AND SNEAK OUT WITHOUT ANYONE NOTICING.
WE'LL PACK FOOD, SLEEPING BAGS, AND SUPPLIES.

HOLD ON TIGHT.
UGH.
I HATE THIS.
COME ON, IT ISN'T SO BAD.
LET'S GO.
STOP!
AH!
THUD!
UGH...
WHAT...?
WHAT ARE YOU DOI—
I KNOW EVERYTHING!
HUH?
I HEARD YOU TALKING THE OTHER DAY!
THIS IS SO WRONG.
YOU'RE TRAITORS!

HOW IS IT POSSIBLE THAT YOU STILL HAVEN'T FOUND THE PRINCESS?!
WE'RE SORRY, YOUR MAJESTY...
WE FOUND THE SOLDIERS THAT WERE WITH HER, BUT THEY CAN'T REMEMBER ANYTHING.
BESIDES, THE WOODS ARE ESPECIALLY DANGEROUS LATELY. WE'VE LOST MANY MEN.
COWARDS!
YOU'RE USELESS! I'LL SEARCH FOR MY DAUGHTER MYSELF.
IF YOU'LL ALLOW ME, MAJESTY... IT'S DANGEROUS.
THE WOODS ARE WITCH TERRITORY THESE DAYS.
AND YOU'RE THEIR PRINCIPAL TARGET.
LET ME GO INSTEAD.
YOU KNOW YOU HAVE MY ABSOLUTE TRUST.
THANK YOU, YOUR MAJESTY.
GO AND FIND MONICA. DON'T DISAPPOINT ME.
MONICA? SURE, I'LL TELL HIM IF I SEE HER.
BUT I HAVE MY PRIORITIES.
IT'S ALMOST THE NEW MOON.

EWW...
THERE ARE TONS OF BUGS.
IT'S GROSS!
OF COURSE, WE'RE IN THE WOODS.
BUGS ARE COOL!
DO YOU NEED HELP?
EVERYTHING'S UNDER CONTROL.
I CAN HANDLE SOME BUGS!
I'M NOT SO SURE...
I HAVE TO OVERCOME MY FEARS OR I WON'T EVER BE A REAL HERO.
ACCORDING TO THE MAP MARK GAVE ME...
...WE'RE CLOSE. WE SHOULD SET UP CAMP BEFORE DUSK.
YESSS, LET'S CAMP!
HOW ROMANTIC.
YOU TWO ARE SO EXCITED.
IT'S LIKE IT'S YOUR FIRST TIME CAMPING.
IT
IS!
I STILL DON'T UNDERSTAND HOW WE GOT HERE...
THE PLAN WAS TO GO TO THE WITCHES' SABBATH WITHOUT RAISING SUSPICION.
BUT...

YOU'RE TRAITORS!
W-WAIT. I CAN EXPL—
GOING ON AN ADVENTURE WITHOUT TELLING ANYONE...
IT'S WRONG TO EXCLUDE US!
THAT'S RIGHT! YOU'RE HURTING OUR FEELINGS!
WE'RE ALL GOING TO WATCH THE METEOR SHOWER. TOGETHER!
AH... FINE.
OH WELL...
SINCE WE'RE HERE...
...I GUESS...
...IT'S BETTER TO HAVE SOME FUN TOGETHER.
HEY, LOOK AT THIS!
IN THE END...
IT'S ME!
WHAT A CUTIE.
BUT YOU SAID THAT IT WAS AN UGLY BIRD.

NOW I THINK IT'S CUTE!
IT'S MY FIRST TIME CAMPING WITH FRIENDS.
WHOA, PRINCESS, THAT REALLY DOES SOUND LIKE YOU.
AARGH!
THIS IS HORRIBLE!
GET OUT OF HERE
YOU DIE
I'M SURE...
UH...
WHAT...?
THIS PLACE...
THIS IS GOING TO BE...
SO MUCH FUN.
DO YOU THINK WITCHES WERE BURNED HERE?
DANI...
LET'S GET OUT OF HERE.
YEAH, LET'S GO.
WE'RE DEFINITELY ON THE RIGHT TRACK...
IT LOOKS LIKE A GOOD PLACE TO CELEBRATE THE SABBATH.

EASY PEASY!
CONGRATULATIONS, DORIAN, YOU'VE JUST RUINED THE FUN OF CAMPING.
YEAH, IT'S BORING THIS WAY.
SIGH... YOU HAVE NO SENSE OF ROMANTICISM.
DON'T WORRY, WE'LL DO THE REST THE OLD-FASHIONED WAY.
OKAY!
...
MONICA, COLLECT SOME FIREWOOD.
OKAY.
AT NIGHT WE CAN TELL HORROR STORIES AROUND THE FIRE!
NICO AND I ARE GOING TO LOOK FOR WATER.
I THINK I HEARD A CREEK, SO IT SHOULDN'T TAKE LONG.
WHAT DO I DO?
STAY HERE AND WATCH THE CAMP.
OKAY! I'LL PROTECT IT WITH MY LIFE!
WHAT ARE YOU DOING?
MARTIAL ARTS.
THOSE AREN'T MARTIAL ARTS!
I'LL TEACH YOU LATER.
OKAY!

IS THIS ENOUGH FIREWOOD?
OUR CAMP IS RIGHT THERE...
I WON'T GO TOO FAR.
HEEEELP!
HUH...?
PLEAAAAASE! GET ME OUT OF HERE!
WHAT'S THAT?
PLEASE! HELP ME!
A GIRL'S VOICE...
HUH?
HEEEELP!

I SWEAR I HEARD A CREEK AROUND HERE...
IT SHOULD BE HERE.
I KNEW I SHOULDN'T HAVE TRUSTED YOU... WE'RE LOST.
SHUT UP, YOU'RE NOT HELPING.
MAYBE WE SHOULD GO BACK...
YOU'RE USING THE MAP UPSIDE DOWN, DUMMY!
DO YOU THINK SO, HONEY?
AH, LOOK! MAYBE WE CAN ASK HER!
HELLO.
DO YOU KNOW HOW TO GET TO THE FLOATING ROCK, BY ANY CHANCE?
WE'RE GOING TO THE WITCHES' SABBATH TOMORROW.
HM?
WHAT?
UM... I DON'T KNOW. I'M SORRY, SIR.
WITCHES' SABBATH...? WHAT WITCHES' SABBATH?
WHAT ARE THESE PEOPLE TALKING ABOUT?

BUT YOU'RE A WITCH, AREN'T YOU? YOU EVEN HAVE THIS LITTLE PET ELF.
I'M NOT A PET ELF!
IF YOU'RE NOT A WITCH... I'LL HAVE TO KILL YOU. MY MISTAKE FOR TELLING YOU ABOUT THE SABBATH.
YES!! I'M A WITCH!
ACTUALLY, HER FACE LOOKS FAMILIAR...
DO YOU THINK SO, HONEY?
MAYBE SHE'S A CLASSMATE OF THE KIDS?
NO, THAT'S NOT IT...
DORIA WYTT
TRAITO
DEAD OR ALI
WYTTE
TRAITOR
D OR ALIVE
IT'S LIKE I'VE SEEN HER FACE RECENTLY...

HELLO?
WHO ARE YOU?
WHAT ARE YOU DOING UP THERE?
I'M THE PRINCESS!
PLEASE, GET ME OUT OF HERE!
WHICH PRINCESS?
AND... HOW CAN I HELP YOU?
WAS A WITCH THE ONE THAT LOCKED YOU UP?
COME UP HERE. ARE YOU MY PRINCE?
...
THERE AREN'T ANY PRINCES LEFT.
BUT DON'T YOU WORRY, I'LL COME GET YOU!
C'MON, MONICA, YOU CAN DO IT!

HERE I GO...
THERE'S NO WAY...
AAAAAAAH! HEEEEEELP!
OKAY.
I CAN DO IT!
IT TOOK ME...
...LONGER THAN...
...I EXPECTED.

...
WHAT?
ARE YOU OKAY?
ER...
PRINCESS?
HUH?
AH!
WHAT IS...?
THAT??

TRAITOR
THERE'S NO DOUBT.
THE WYTTES ARE TRAITORS... WHO WOULD HAVE THOUGHT?
WHAT DO WE DO? DO WE TAKE HER TO THE SABBATH?
IT'S HER.
DANIELA WYTTE
DANIELA WYTTE.
I HEARD THAT SHE AND HER BROTHER TRIED TO STEAL A DRAGON EGG.
A DRAGON EGG? DO WE HAVE DRAGONS?! HOW COOL!
THAT'S NOT THE POINT. WHAT DO WE DO WITH HER?
WE BRING HER, RIGHT?
IT SAYS THAT THEY WANT HER DEAD OR ALIVE...
SHE'S JUST A KID. WHO WOULD WANT TO KILL A KID?
MAYBE THEY WANT TO SACRIFICE HER ON THE PYRE.
WHAT ARE YOU SAYING? BURN HER?!
SHE'S ONE OF US! WE CAN'T DO THAT!

SO WHAT'S YOUR SUGGESTION? LET HER GO?
I DON'T KNOW.
WE DON'T EVEN KNOW WHAT WILL HAPPEN AT THE WITCHES' SABBATH...
IT'S OBVIOUS! IT'S CLEAR—
HEY! WHERE IS SHE?
SHE'S RUNNING AWAY!
GO CATCH HER!
WHAT DO WE DO?! SHOULD WE FOLLOW HER?
OF COURSE! WHAT ARE YOU WAITING FOR?
GO YOURSELF!
I'M NOT GOING TO CHASE HER THROUGH THE WOODS! MY MOTHER IS WAITING IN THE CAR.
EXCUSE ME... WHAT'S ALL THE FUSS ABOUT?
IT LOOKS LIKE THEY FOUND WYTTE'S DAUGHTER...
SHE'S ACCUSED OF TREASON FOR SOME INCIDENT WITH A DRAGON'S EGG...
HUH?
WYTTE?
DOESN'T RING A BELL? THEY'RE PRETTY FAMOUS.
NOT AT ALL.

REALLY? DO YOU LIVE UNDER A ROCK OR SOMETHING?
THE WYTTES ARE A VERY FAMOUS FAMILY IN THE WORLD OF WITCHES.
THEY'VE BEEN ORGANIZING THE SABBATH.
YOU IDIOTS.
WHAT?
YOU'RE HOLDING UP TRAFFIC. LEAVE THE KID ALONE AND KEEP IT MOVING.
SHUT YOUR MOUTH! SHE'S A TRAITOR!
ACCORDING TO WHOM?
ISN'T HER FAMILY BEHIND THE SABBATH?
YES, BUT—
YOU'RE A BUNCH OF IDIOTS.
IT'S OBVIOUS THAT SOMEONE WANTS TO GET RID OF THE WYTTES.
WHATEVER.
I'M GOING AFTER THE GIRL.
ONCE WE'RE AT THE FLOATING ROCK, THEY CAN DECIDE WHAT TO DO WI—
RIBBIT

WHOA! WHAT WAS THAT?
I HAVE NO IDEA.
BUT IT SEEMS LIKE WE LOST THEM.
THAT WAS CLOSE.
WHY WERE THEY ACCUSING YOU OF BEING A TRAITOR?
DORIAN GRABBED A DRAGON EGG WHEN WE WERE AT THE PRISON ON THE FLOATING ROCK.
BUT HE DROPPED IT BEFORE WE LEFT.
I DIDN'T THINK THEY WOULD TAKE IT SO SERIOUSLY.
I THINK WE'RE GOING THE WRONG WAY.
OUR CAMP IS IN THE OPPOSITE DIRECTION.
WE'RE NOT GOING BACK TO CAMP.
I DON'T WANT TO PUT THE OTHERS IN DANGER.
WHAT?!
DORIAN COULD PULVERIZE THOSE IDIOTS IN A SECOND!
YOU'RE WRONG, NICO.
GROWN-UP WITCHES ARE POWERFUL...
WE CAN'T BEAT THEM. IT'S BETTER TO RUN.

IT'S BEEN...
...A LONG TIME...
...SINCE I RAN LIKE THIS.
I THINK WE'RE LOST...
...AND IT'S PITCH BLACK OUT HERE.
COULD YOU CAST SOME LIGHT WITH YOUR WAND?
I DON'T HAVE MY WAND ANYMORE. I GAVE IT TO DORIAN.
WHAT? WHY?!
HE'LL MAKE BETTER USE OF IT.
HE LOST HIS IN THE WOODS THE DAY...
...YOU KNOW...
THEY ALMOST BURNED ME ALIVE.
ANYWAY, EVERY TIME I TRY TO CAST A SPELL, I HURT SOMEONE.
I'VE DECIDED TO STOP DOING MAGIC.
DORIAN DOESN'T KNOW YET, SO DON'T TELL HIM.
I'M SURE HE'LL GET MAD, BUT I'D RATHER TELL HIM MYSELF.
BUT DANI... THIS ISN'T RIGHT.
YOU—
DON'T WORRY. I *WILL* GET YOU BACK TO YOUR ORIGINAL SIZE.
IT'LL BE THE LAST SPELL I CAST.
I PROMISE.

...
OKAY, COME ON...
YOU CAN DO THIS.
IF DANI CAN DO IT, SO CAN YOU.
RELAX, MONICA...
YOU'VE GOT THIS.
JUST ONE MORE STEP AND—
AAAAAAAH!!
I CAN'T. IT'S IMPOSSIBLE!
HOW AM I SUPPOSED TO GET DOWN?
THEY'RE TAKING FOREVER...
CARLO! KEEP AN EYE ON THE CAMP!

...
NOTHING.
NOT A SINGLE TRAP DOOR.
HOW AM I GOING TO GET OUT OF HERE?
I HAVE TO FIND A WAY.
IT'S SO DARK... AND COLD...
AND...
WHAT IF THE WITCH WHO CAST THAT SPELL COMES BACK?
BECAUSE IT HAD TO BE A WITCH WHO CURSED THAT DOLL. RIGHT?
WHAT IF SHE TURNS *ME* INTO A DOLL?!
HELLO?
MONICA?!
HUH?
DORIAN! UP HERE!
UP HERE!
HUH...?
WHAT ARE YOU DOING UP THERE?
THERE WAS A GIRL YELLING. BUT IT WAS A TRAP!
I CLIMBED UP HERE TO SAVE HER BUT NOW I DON'T KNOW HOW TO GET DOWN!
I THINK THAT THIS WHOLE THING WAS MADE BY A WITCH!
BUT ARE YOU OKAY?!
IS THE WITCH WITH YOU?
I'M FINE! I'M ALONE!
GLAD TO HEAR IT.

BUT I'M STUCK.
THERE'S NO DOOR?
AHA! I HAVE AN IDEA.
CATCH!
A BROOM?
I'M NOT SURE I—
GO FIND DANI!
SHE'LL FLY UP TO GET ME.
I'LL GET ON THE BROOM WITH HER!
IT'S THE ONLY WAY OUT.
IT MIGHT BE A WHILE. JUST WAIT THERE!
WHERE DO YOU EXPECT ME TO GO?
OKAY, I'LL FIND HER.
BUT SHE'S BEEN GONE FOR HOURS, TOO.

RUN, DORIAN!
FASTER!
FASTER!
YOU NEED DANI TO—
IT'S A GOOD THING THAT DORIAN FOUND ME.
OTHERWISE, I WOULD HAVE STAYED HERE, STUCK IN THE DARK.
I RAN AWAY FROM HOME TO SAVE WILL
BUT I CAN'T EVEN SAVE MYSELF.

ALL I'M GOOD FOR IS WAITING FOR SOMEONE ELSE TO RESCUE ME.
LIKE EVERY OTHER STUPID DAMSEL IN DISTRESS.
KNOCK
HUH?
KNOCK
WHAT IS THAT?
KNOCK
IS IT THE WITCH...
KNOCK
COMING TO GET ME?
KNOCK
KNOCK

DORIAN!
HEY!
YOU'RE FLYING!
HOW...?
QUICK, GET ON.
LET'S GET OUT OF HERE!

GIVE ME A SECOND.
DON'T LET GO.
I WON'T.
STUPID BROOM...
COME CLOSER.
I'M TRYING! BUT I CAN'T CONTROL IT...
DORIAN, CATCH ME.
WHAT?!
AAH!
WHAT ARE YOU DOING?!
SEE?
DONE!
LET'S GO.
HOLD ON TIGHT.
AAAAAAAH!

QUICK, TURN!
A-ARE YOU SURE?
WE'RE GONNA CRASH!
NO WAY—
LOOK, THAT WAY!
GO DOWN A LITTLE...
DON'T LET GO!
PUFF!

IT...
HURTS...
I'M SORRY...
I SHOULDN'T HAVE TRIED TO RIDE THE BROOM.
YOU WERE GREAT!
REALLY?
YES!
FLYING IS EVEN MORE FUN THAN I THOUGHT.
WE MAKE A GREAT TEAM!
I STILL DON'T LIKE FLYING THE BROOM.
CLAP
BUT YOU HELPED ME ANYWAY.
THANK YOU.
YOU'RE WELCOME.
AND...
UH...
...
WELL, I...
WHAT?
...
NOTHING.
FORGET ABOUT IT.
LET'S GO.

HEY, MONICA...
BEFORE, WHEN I CAME UP TO THE TOWER...
WHY WERE YOU CRYING?
I WASN'T CRYING!
RE- REALLY...
BUT...
YOU WERE RIGHT FROM THE BEGINNING,
WHEN YOU SAID I WAS JUST A PRINCESS PRETENDING TO BE A HERO.
I WASN'T SERIOUS.
BUT IT'S TRUE. I CAN'T EVEN SAVE MYSELF.
I'M SORRY I GOT SO MAD. YOU WERE TELLING THE TRUTH.
I'M JUST WASTING TIME, WHILE WILL MIGHT...
HE MIGHT ALREADY BE DEAD.
DON'T SAY THAT!
YOU'RE NOT WASTING TIME, YOU'RE LEARNING HOW TO FIGHT.
I HAVEN'T LEARNED ANYTHING USEFUL.
I GOT STICK IN THAT TOWER. I'M RIDICULOUS.
YOU'RE NOT RIDICULOUS.
YOU CLIMBED UP THERE WITHOUT HESITATING TO SAVE SOMEONE.
THAT SOUNDS PRETTY HEROIC TO ME.
MAYBE.
BUT I GOT STUCK THERE LIKE A FOOL. THAT'S THE PROBLEM.
MONICA, I WOULDN'T HAVE KNOWN HOW TO GET DOWN FROM THERE EITHER.
WHAT ARE YOU TALKING ABOUT?
YOU FLEW UP AND SAVED ME.
BUT I WASN'T ALONE.

CHAPTER 14

WE'RE A GREAT TEAM.
RIGHT?
...
THEN...
COULD YOU TEACH ME MAGIC?
YES.
THAT WAS FAST.
HUH?
REALLY?
I MEAN... IT'S EXCITING.
AFTER ALL, YOU SAID WITCHES WERE SERVANTS OF THE DEVIL WHEN I FIRST MET YOU.
BY THE WAY, CALL ME PROFESSOR WYTTE FROM NOW ON.
NO WAY!
DO YOU WANT ME TO TEACH YOU OR NOT?
HEY!
AH!
HEY, LOOK AT THAT.
IT'S SO PRETTY!

QUICK, MAKE A WISH!
WE CAN MAKE A TON.
WHOA.
!
DANI!
WHAT ARE YOU DOING DOWN THERE?
...DANI?
WHAT IS SHE LOOKING AT?
DANI! WHAT'S WRONG?
HAVE YOU SEEN THE SHOOTING STARS?
LOOK...
HUH?
WHO ARE ALL THOSE PEOPLE?

THEY'RE WITCHES, RIGHT? WHERE ARE THEY GOING?
MONICA, THE TRUTH IS THAT WE—
I DON'T KNOW.
HUH?
BUT I DON'T THINK IT'S A GOOD IDEA TO STAY HERE.
THEY COULD BE EVIL WITCHES, LIKE MASTER ALWAYS TALKS ABOUT.
THE WITCH THAT SET YOUR TRAP COULD BE AMONG THEM.
ISN'T IT DANGEROUS TO BE SPENDING THE NIGHT IN THE WOODS?
I DON'T THINK SO. THEY'RE ALL GOING THE SAME WAY...
BESIDES, WE HAVE TO SEE THE METEOR SHOWER TOGETHER!
THAT'S RIGHT! LET'S KEEP THE PARTY GOING.
THERE'S NO REASON TO ASSUME THEY'RE ALL EVIL.
LET'S WISH ON ALL THE STARS!
HOW?
YOU JUST MAKE A WISH WHEN YOU SEE A SHOOTING STAR. PRETTY EASY RIGHT NOW!
DORIAN, WAIT.
AREN'T YOU GOING TO TELL THEM THAT WE'RE GOING TO THE WITCHES' SABBATH TOMORROW?
DO YOU STILL WANT TO GO?
I HAVE THE FEELING THAT HE CHANGED HIS MIND.

EITHER WAY, I'M GLAD...
SCARY STORY TIME!
HA! I'M AN EXPERT! I BET MY STORY WILL BE THE MOST TERRIFYING.
LET'S HAVE A COMPETITION THEN.
IN THE END, EVEN THOUGH THERE WERE SOME BAD TIMES...
...CAMPING HAS BEEN A BLAST.
ALL TOGETHER.
I DIDN'T KNOW THAT SLEEPING IN THE WOODS COULD BE SO GREAT.
ALTHOUGH I GUESS THAT...
WHEN YOU'RE WITH YOUR FRIENDS...
EVERYTHING IS MORE FUN.

HEY, DANI, WAKE UP.
DORIAN...?
WHAT ARE YOU DOING HERE?
GET DRESSED AND COME OUT. BUT DON'T MAKE ANY NOISE.
WHY ARE YOU UP AT THIS HOUR?
TO GO TO THE WITCHES' SABBATH, OF COURSE.
WHAT?! DIDN'T YOU CHANGE YOUR MIND?!
THIS IS THE WHOLE REASON WE CAME, REMEMBER?
I JUST DON'T WANT TO PUT THE OTHERS IN DANGER.
COME ON, GET ON.
NO.
FINE.
I'LL GO ALONE.
NO! WAIT!
YOU DON'T KNOW HOW TO RIDE THE BROOM!
POW
DORIAN...
WHY ARE YOU SO FOCUSED ON THE SABBATH?
I KNOW YOU'RE SCARED.
BUT IT'S OUR DUTY AS WITCHES TO FIND OUT WHAT'S GOING ON IN OUR COMMUNITY.

OUR COMMUNITY?
WE'RE NOT WELCOME THERE ANYMORE. THEY CONSIDER US TRAITORS.
WHAT?!
I WAS ALMOST ARRESTED BY SOME WITCHES TODAY.
WHY DIDN'T YOU TELL ME BEFORE?
BECAUSE THESE THINGS BOTHER YOU A LOT.
I DIDN'T WANT TO WORRY YOU
BUT DANI—
LET ME GO!
ARE YOU NOT HAPPY TO FINALLY HAVE FRIENDS?
WHY ARE YOU NOT CONTENT WITH BEING NORMAL AND LIVING PEACEFULLY?
LET'S GO BACK TO NICO AND MONICA.
DO YOU WANT TO GO BACK TO THE MASTER'S HOUSE LIKE NOTHING HAPPENED?
THEN WHAT?
WHAT ARE YOU GOING TO DO WHEN A WAR STARTS AND THEY COME TO KILL US?
WHO'S GOING TO KILL US, DORIAN?
ORDINARY PEOPLE? OR WITCHES?
WHO ARE YOU AFRAID OF?
...
I DON'T KNOW, DANI.
THAT'S WHAT I WANT TO GO FIGURE OUT.

CHAPTER 15

THE FIRST TIME I SAW HIM
I PRESENT TO YOU...PRINCE WILLIAM.
YOUR FIANCÉ.
I THOUGHT HE WAS THE LIVING IMAGE
OF A PRINCE CHARMING.
HIS BEARING AND ELEGANCE,
THE SELF-CONFIDENCE HE RADIATED...
I WAS IMPRESSED.
BUT NOT FOR TOO LONG.
CRASH
IT WAS HER.
HUH?!
WILL, I SAW YOU!
IS IT REALLY NECESSARY FOR WILLIAM TO LIVE HERE?
WITCH HUNTING IS IN THE PAST NOW. IT'S FORBIDDEN.
YOU SHOULD BE GRATEFUL THAT I'M WILLING TO FORGE THIS ALLIANCE INSTEAD OF JAILING YOU, EDGAR.
THAT WITCH DESERVED TO DIE.
YOU'D DO WELL TO REMEMBER THAT YOUR SON IS UNDER MY ROOF BEFORE BREAKING THE LAW.

I REALIZED QUICKLY
THAT WILLIAM WASN'T AN ATHLETE.
OR A SCHOLAR.
IN WHICH YEAR DID THE NORTH TERRITORIES INVADE?
IN 532.
AFTER QUEEN CRISTINA'S DEATH, A LONG TERM OF POLITICAL INSECURITY BEGAN...
WHY?
THEY DIDN'T KNOW WHO TO VOTE FOR.
WHO FORBADE THE WITCHES' SABBATH AND WHY?
SAINT PATRICK'S KNIGHT.
BECAUSE THEY WERE TOO LOUD AND DISTURBED THE NEIGHBORS.
INCREDIBLE...
YOU DIDN'T GET A SINGLE ONE RIGHT!
HUH?
WHY DO I HAVE TO LEARN ALL THIS BORING STUFF, ANYWAY?
I'M A PRINCE, NOT A TEACHER.
IF YOU LEARN ALL THIS, IT'LL BE EASIER TO FIGHT AGAINST THE WITCHES.
I DON'T *WANT* TO FIGHT AGAINST THEM!
I THINK WE SHOULD ALL LEARN SOME MAGIC, INSTEAD.
WHAT? DON'T BE A FOOL. MAGIC IS EVIL.
NO, IT WOULD BE AWESOME. RIGHT?
WE SHOULD STUDY.
IDIOT...

BUT HE WAS DETERMINED TO BE THE PERFECT PRINCE.
PRINCE WILLIAM IS RIDICULOUS AGAIN!
BUT HE'S SO CLUMSY.
I THINK HE'S CUTE.
I THINK IT'S COOL THAT HE'S TRYING SO HARD.
YOU TOO?!
HE'S NOT COOL AT ALL!
THIS IS...
...TERRIFYING.
MOM IS WAITING FOR ME ON THE STAIRS TO INTRODUCE ME TO SOCIETY.
I CAN'T GO OUT THERE.
HEY.
WILL.
SAVE ME!
FIRST TIME AT A BALL?
YEP.
LEAVE IT TO ME, MONICA!
JUST PUT ON A COMPLETELY SERIOUS FACE.
YOU MUST LOOK CONFIDENT AND FORMAL.
WON'T THEY REALIZE I'M PRETENDING?
EVERYONE HERE IS PRETENDING.
LIKE THAT GUY OVER THERE.
HE PLAYS THE PIANO AT EVERY PARTY EVEN THOUGH HE'S TERRIBLE.

EVERYONE KNOWS IT, BUT WE ALL APPLAUD.
STOP OR I'LL LAUGH!
I KNOW YOU'RE JUST SAYING ALL THAT TO CALM ME DOWN.
THE DEVIL'S SMILE
NO, I JUST LOVE GOSSIP.
WE GOT ALONG VERY WELL. WE WERE ALWAYS SPENDING TIME TOGETHER.
AND WE LOVED EACH OTHER.
A LOT.
BUT...
...I DISCOVERED ROMANTIC NOVELS.
Dusk
Dusk
ROMERO & JULIA
PRINCESS, WE'RE GOING ON A PICNIC. ARE YOU COMING?
MONICA, I FELL OFF MY HORSE AND BROKE MY ARM.
WANT TO SIGN MY CAST?
HONEY, I THINK YOU SHOULD GO OUT AND GET SOME SUN. YOU'RE LOOKING A BIT PALE...
PRINCESS, PRINCE WILLIAM HAS ASKED ME TO TELL YOU THAT HE'S IN SERIOUS DANGER AND MAY DIE.
YOU MUST GO RESCUE HIM.
ALL THOSE BOOKS OPENED MY EYES.
I MUST FIND MY TRUE LOVE.
I WANT YOU TO ANNUL MY ENGAGEMENT WITH WILLIAM.
WHAT?
YOU'RE FORCING US TO MARRY EACH OTHER AGAINST OUR WILL. IT'S SO OLD-FASHIONED!
RIGHT, WILL?
I GUESS.
I WANT TO MARRY FOR LOVE!

SO I STARTED MEETING OTHER PRINCES.
HAVE YOU SEEN THESE MUSCLES, PRINCESS?
UGH...
SCARY!
HER LOSS.
IT'D BE MY PLEASURE TO MARRY YOU, PRINCESS MONICA.
MY SISTER CAN TEACH YOU ALL ABOUT MY INTERESTS SO YOU CAN TAKE THEM UP, TOO.
WHAT?
NO THANKS!
WAS IT SOMETHING I SAID?
YOU'RE A FOOL, BROTHER.
BUT NONE OF THEM WERE MY TRUE LOVE.
SO, I EXPANDED MY DATING POOL.
HI, WILL!
HAVE YOU FOUND YOUR TRUE LOVE YET?
OF COURSE!
REALLY? WHO?
HUH?
WELL...
?
AHA! HERE THEY ARE!
WHAT ARE YOU DOING?
SLAP!
CUTE!
I CAN'T BELIEVE YOU.
AND THEN I MET HIM.
HE'S SO HANDSOME AND MYSTERIOUS.

WHO ARE YOU GRINNING AT, YOU SILLY GIRL?
HUH? WHAT'S HAPPENING?
WHAT DO YOU THINK IS HAPPENING?
LOOK AROUND—
I THOUGHT YOU WERE MY TRUE LOVE.
HA! VAIN, AS I EXPECTED. YOUR DAD ORDERED MY FATHER'S BURNING.
I FOOLED YOU. NOW, I'M TAKING MY REVENGE.
I'LL SHOW YOU WHAT A WITCH CAN DO...
STOP, VILLAIN!
WHO ARE YOU?
WILL!
WHOAAA!
AAARGH!
MONICA! ARE YOU ALL RIGHT?
I COULDN'T FIND MY TRUE LOVE.
BUT WHEN I WAS WITH WILL...
I FELT AT HOME.

WHEN WILL DISAPPEARED, I FELT COMPLETELY HELPLESS.
IT TOOK ME A WEEK TO GO OUT AND LOOK FOR HIM.
A WEEK THAT I SPENT CRYING IN MY BED.
I PROMISED MYSELF THAT I WOULD NEVER ALLOW MYSELF TO LOSE SOMEONE THAT I LOVED AGAIN.
ar Monica and Nico,
n sorry. I lied when I said I didn't know
here all those witches were going.
are attending an important witches'
sabbath.
Dani and I have decided to go.
We need to see what's happening.
Please, be careful. Witches are
rous. Or that's what I think
ack home and tell the master
that I'm really sorry. Don't worry
about us, I would never let
anything bad happen to Dani again.
I'm sorry,
Dorian.
BUT NOW I HAVE.
WE SHOULD GO GET MASTER PENDRAGON.
MAYBE THE MASTER'S RIGHT AND WE CAN'T TRUST THEM...
PRINCESS!
WHERE ARE YOU GOING?
I DON'T KNOW IF I'VE GROWN UP, OR MATURED, OR IF I'M JUST FOOLING MYSELF.
BUT I DO KNOW THAT THIS TIME...
THEY CAN'T HAVE GOTTEN FAR.
WE'RE GOING TO FIND THEM.
I'M NOT GOING TO WAIT FOR A WEEK.

CHAPTER 16

THIS IS TOO DANGEROUS! I THINK IT'D BE BETTER IF WE GO GET THE MASTER.
IF IT'S THAT DANGEROUS, DORIAN AND DANI MIGHT BE IN DANGER TOO.
YOU SAID THEY'RE WANTED FOR TREASON, RIGHT?
YES, BUT—
BESIDES, YOU'RE MY BODYGUARD, REMEMBER? I'M COUNTING ON YOU!
BUT...
PRINCESS—
LET'S GO!
THE CARS ARE STOPPED...
I HAVE AN IDEA.
THIS WILL DO!
THIS VAN SMELLS TERRIBLE.
WE'RE GONNA GET CAUGHT!
I DON'T UNDERSTAND WHY SO MANY PEOPLE ARE COMING TO THIS STUPID SABBATH.
FOR THE SAME REASON WE ARE: SO WE AREN'T LABELED TRAITORS.
WE'VE BEEN STOPPED FOR *TWO HOURS.*
UHH... GUYS?
IT LOOKS LIKE WE HAVE A STOWAWAY.
HUH?!
A WITCH?
I DON'T THINK SO, HER CLOTHES ARE PRETTY WEIRD.
MY CLOTHES ARE WEIRD?!
...
I MEAN, BLACK IS MANDATORY FOR THE SABBATH. A WITCH WOULD KNOW THAT.

OF COURSE I KNEW!
I JUST DECIDED NOT TO FOLLOW THE RULES BECAUSE I'M SO POWERFUL.
IS THAT A WAND? IT LOOKS LIKE A TWIG.
OF COURSE IT'S A WAND!!
I DON'T THINK YOU CAN DO ANYTHING WITH THAT THING.
NO? THEN HOW DID I DO THIS TO THE LAST PERSON WHO DARED INSULT ME?
WHAT?
AWWWW, WHAT A CUTIE PIE!
THIS IS WHAT YOU SAID I'M USEFUL FOR?
NOBODY CAN RETURN HIM TO HIS NORMAL SIZE BECAUSE MY POWER IS SO AWESOME.
SERIOUSLY? LET ME TRY!
I WANT TO TRY TOO.
STOP!
NO MORE EXPERIMENTING ON MY PIXIE!
NO FAIR!
WHICH SPELL DID YOU USE TO SHRINK HIM?
UH, A VERY FAMOUS SPELL, YES...
WAS IT AN ALTERATION SPELL OR A TRANSMUTATION SPELL?
UH...

YOU'RE NOT A WITCH, ARE YOU?
...
GIRL, YOU'RE A TERRIBLE ACTRESS! YOU WEREN'T FOOLING ANYONE.
ARE YOU GOING TO KILL ME?
WHAT?!
ARE YOU GOING TO BURN ME AS A SACRIFICE OR SOMETHING?
WHAT ARE YOU TALKING ABOUT? DO WE LOOK LIKE MURDERERS?!
WELL...
NO, WE HAVE NOTHING AGAINST NON-MAGIC PEOPLE.
BUT THIS ISN'T THE SAFEST PLACE FOR YOU TO BE...
YOU'LL HAVE TO BE MORE CAREFUL NOT TO BE RECOGNIZED.
THERE ARE SOME CRAZY WITCHES HERE.
I'M LOOKING FOR MY FRIENDS. THEY'RE WITCHES AND TOLD ME THEY WERE GOING TO THE SABBATH.
I WANT TO FIND THEM. THEN I'LL LEAVE.
GOOD IDEA.
SO THEN...
WHY ARE YOU GOING TO THE SABBATH IF THESE WITCHES ARE SO EVIL?

THEY SENT A LETTER TO ALL THE WITCHES FROM NEIGHBORING KINGDOMS
SAYING THAT IF WE DIDN'T ATTEND, WE WOULD BE BRANDED TRAITORS.
AND IF YOU'RE CONSIDERED A TRAITOR BY THESE PEOPLE, YOU'RE AS GOOD AS DEAD.
WHICH PEOPLE?
THE BIGWIGS WHO RUN THE FLOATING ROCK.
THE WYTTE FAMILY ARE THE MOST FAMOUS.
THEY'RE TERRIFYING.
THEY WANT TO TAKE OVER THE COUNTRY. YEAH, AND KILL THE KING TO PUT A WITCH IN HIS PLACE.
WHAT...?
THEY WANT REVENGE ON NORMAL PEOPLE, TOO.
YOU KNOW, FOR ALL THE WITCH BURNING...
NO... THAT'S NOT... POSSIBLE.
DUDES, WE'RE HERE!
PUT YOUR HATS ON.
FIRST... WE'LL DO A LITTLE MAKEOVER.
SO YOU DON'T GET KILLED WHILE YOU LOOK FOR YOUR FRIENDS!
WHAT? WHY??
ADMIT IT, ALEX, YOU JUST LIKE STYLING HAIR.
YES, THAT TOO.
LET ME HELP YOU.
HOW PRETTY!
YOU'RE NOT SUSPICIOUS AT ALL, NOW.

ARE YOU SURE?
WHAT...
IS THAT?
THE FLOATING ROCK. THE WITCH'S PRISON!
LOTS OF WITCHES USED TO LIVE IN THIS FOREST. THE PRISON WAS USED TO LOCK THEM UP.
THE GUARDS SAY THAT WE HAVE TO GO UP ONE BY ONE ON OUR OWN BROOMS. NO SHARING.
THEN WE HAVE TO CAST THE OATH SPELL.
WHAT? BUT...
I CAN'T RIDE A BROOM!
YOU'LL HAVE TO TRY.
IS THERE A PROBLEM?
ZERO PROBLEMS, SIR!
YOU CAN USE THIS BROOM. HAVE YOU FLOWN BEFORE?
BUT...
YE-YESTERDAY.
PERFECT! IF YOU'VE DONE IT BEFORE, IT'LL BE EASY PEASY.
BECAUSE YOU ALREADY KNOW YOU CAN DO IT!
BUT... I WASN'T ALONE.
WE'LL WAIT FOR YOU UP THERE!
PRINCESS, IT'S NOT LOOKING GOOD.

I CAN'T DO IT...
THEY'RE GONNA CATCH ME.
MAYBE NICO IS RIGHT...
AND THE BEST THING WE CAN DO
IS GO LOOK FOR HELP...
BUT...
ALL RIGHT, WE'LL FIGHT TOGETHER!
WE'RE A GREAT TEAM. RIGHT?
...
I CAN DO THIS.
WHOA!

I'M FLYING.
MONICA!
WHA...?!
WHAT ARE YOU DOING HERE?
OW.
MASTER?!
YOU SHOULDN'T BE HERE.
WHERE ARE DANI AND DORIAN?

THEY'RE PROBABLY ON THE FLOATING ROCK ALREADY.
NICO, HOW COULD YOU LET THIS HAPPEN?
BUT—
YOUR ONLY JOB WAS TO KEEP AN EYE ON THEM.
YOU'VE LET ME DOWN.
NOW IT'S TOO LATE.
I SHOULD HAVE KILLED THEM WHEN I HAD THE CHANCE.
IF THEY ARE ALREADY WITH THE OTHERS...
WE'RE ALL DEAD.
WE'RE ALREADY HERE! IT'S BEEN SO LONG.
YEAH.
WHAT'S WRONG, DORIAN?
I DON'T KNOW IF WE'RE DOING THE RIGHT THING...
MAYBE MOM AND DAD ARE AT THE WITCHES' SABBATH ALREADY.
IF THEY'RE NOT HOME, WE CAN ALWAYS GO TO THE SABBATH.
AND IF THEY'RE HOME...
THEY'LL KNOW WHAT TO DO.
AT LEAST I CAN GET A BETTER WAND AT HOME.
HAVEN'T YOU LOOKED IN YOUR BAG?
WHAT?
NOTHING...
BUT MAKE SURE YOU KEEP YOUR BAG WITH YOU, OKAY?

WHAT DO YOU MEAN...
WE'RE DEAD?
IT'S A LONG STORY...
IT STARTS ABOUT SIX MONTHS AGO.
AT THE TIME, SOME RUMORS ABOUT A WITCH REBELLION STARTED...
A REBELLION AGAINST KINGS AND PEOPLE WHO DON'T PRACTICE MAGIC.
I STARTED GETTING SCARED.
I HAD DEDICATED YEARS OF MY LIFE TO IMPROVING THE REPUTATION OF WITCHES...
I LIVED WITH NORMAL PEOPLE AND HELPED THEM WITH MY MAGIC.
I DIDN'T WANT THAT PEACE BEING THREATENED BY VINDICTIVE WITCHES.
I SPENT HOURS IN FRONT OF MY CRYSTAL BALL, TRYING TO SEE SOMETHING THAT WOULD GUIDE ME...
FINALLY, I SAW IT.
WHAT?
I'M AN AVERAGE WITCH.
I'M NOT ESPECIALLY POWERFUL.
BUT THERE'S ONE THING I'M REALLY GOOD AT,
STATION
AND IT'S SEEING THE FUTURE.

EVERYTHING I SEE COMES TO PASS.
AND WHAT I SAW...
WAS MORE HORRIBLE THAN I COULD HAVE EVER IMAGINED.
I SAW A WORLD DESTROYED BY WAR.
A DEVASTATED WORLD FULL OF FIRE, DEATH, AND REVENGE.
A WORLD WHERE THE WITCHES WERE WINNING,
AND EVERYONE ELSE WAS FIGHTING FOR THEIR LIVES. WITH NO SUCCESS.
AND I SAW A PERSON
STATION
CITY HALL
CASTLE
CEMETERY
LEADING ALL THIS CHAOS, BRUTAL AND RUTHLESS.
A PERSON WHO THE WITCHES FOLLOWED BLINDLY.
THAT PERSON WAS THE KING OF THE WITCHES,
WHO WILL BE SELECTED TODAY AT THE WITCHES' SABBATH.

IT WAS SOMEONE VERY YOUNG.
SKINNY, WITH FAIR SKIN.
DARK HAIR AND EYES,
DRESSED COMPLETELY IN BLACK.
THEY WERE WEARING A BLACK CROWN, FLYING THROUGH THE SKIES.
I SAW THEIR FACE.
THERE'S NO DOUBT.
THE KING OF THE WITCHES IS ONE OF THEM.
TRAITORS
DORIAN...
...OR DANI.

YOU'RE LYING.
DORIAN AND DANI WOULD NEVER HURT ANYONE!!
I SAW THEIR FACE. I KNOW IT'S ONE OF THEM.
THE WYTTES ARE EXTREMELY POWERFUL.
IT WOULDN'T SURPRISE ME IF THE WITCHES CHOSE ONE OF THEM AS THEIR NEW LEADER.
DORIAN CAN EXECUTE ANY SPELL ON HIS FIRST TRY.
DANI DOES THINGS NO ONE ELSE CAN UNDO.
I'VE NEVER SEEN ANYTHING LIKE THEM.
BUT MASTER... WHY DIDN'T YOU DO ANYTHING BACK THEN?
I TRIED.
I DIDN'T KNOW HOW TO GET TO THEM WITHOUT RAISING THE ALARM.
WHEN THEY MISSED THE BUS TO SCHOOL, I SAW MY CHANCE.
I TRIED TO LURE THEM TO ME AS APPRENTICES, BUT THEY IGNORED MY ADVERTISEMENTS.
EARCHIN
APPRENT
UNTIL THE DAY THEY CAME TO ME.
MY IDEA WAS TO POISON THEM BEFORE THEY COULD DO ANY HARM, BUT...

I COULDN'T. AFTER ALL, THEY WERE JUST KIDS.
BESIDES, ONLY ONE OF THEM WOULD BE THE FUTURE KING.
INSTEAD OF COMMITTING MURDER, I THOUGHT IT BETTER TO EDUCATE THEM.
PREVENT THEM FROM TURNING INTO SOMETHING TERRIBLE.
I THOUGHT IT WORKED... THINGS SEEMED CALMER.
BUT I WAS WRONG.
NOW...
I DON'T KNOW WHAT TO DO.
ARE YOU PLANNING TO KILL THEM?
NO...
I DON'T KNOW.
I MIGHT BE TOO LATE.
IT'S NOT TOO LATE!
YOU SAID IT YOURSELF: DORIAN AND DANI ARE GOOD!
WE JUST HAVE TO GO UP TO THE FLOATING ROCK AND BRING THEM HOME!
I HOPE YOU'RE RIGHT, PRINCESS.

AND WHO'LL BE PROPOSED AS THE NEW KING?
WILL THERE BE AN ELECTION OR SOMETHING?
HEY, I'LL VOTE FOR YOU!
HAHA
WHERE ARE THE PRISONERS KEPT?
WHAT?
THE PRINCES. WHERE ARE THEY?
HEY, YOU!
YOU CAN'T BE HERE. SABBATH IS IN THE MAIN HALL.

HUH?
YOU'LL BE SORRY.
I NEED REINFORCEMENTS!
WHAT'S WRONG THERE?
ARE YOU GOING TO TELL ME WHERE THEY ARE...
OR NOT?

...
DAMIEN?
IS THAT YOU?
WILL!
HOLD ON...
WHOAA!
IT'S BEEN SO LONG!
HUH?
YOU FINALLY CAME!
YEAH.
I'M GLAD YOU'RE ALL RIGHT.
ME TOO. BUT WHAT TOOK YOU SO LONG?
I DIDN'T KNOW WHERE THEY WERE KEEPING YOU.
BUT HEY,
I BROUGHT YOU THIS.
MY SWORD!

I ALSO GRABBED SOME OF THE GUARDS' UNIFORMS SO WE CAN SNEAK OUT.
IF THEY CATCH US, WE'RE DONE.
KEEP CALM, GUYS. I'LL GET US OUT OF HERE.
YAAAY!
BRAVO, WILLIAM!
YOU'RE AWESOME.
SHOULD I TELL THEM THAT HE'S ACTUALLY A DISASTER?
IT'S DUSK. WHAT ARE WE WAITING FOR?
NOTHING. LET'S GO.
GOOD EVENING, EVERYONE!
THANK YOU FOR ATTENDING THE WITCHES' SABBATH, WHICH WILL BEGIN A NEW ERA.
WE'VE ARRIVED JUST IN TIME.
HUH?
NICO??
MASTER, NICO FELL FROM MY SHOULDER!
TELL ME YOU AREN'T SERIOUS...
CALM DOWN, I'M RIGHT HERE!

NICO! YOU'RE BACK TO YOUR NORMAL SIZE.
NEW MOON, REMEMBER? I CAN BE YOUR BODYGUARD AGAIN!
LIKE MY HAT? I STOLE IT.
SHH.
LISTEN UP. WE HAVE NO TIME TO LOSE!
AS YOU ALREADY KNOW, OUR PRIORITY IS TO DESTROY THE KING
AND CROWN A WITCH IN HIS PLACE.
AND WHAT IS THE BEST WAY TO CHOOSE ONE'S MONARCH?
MAGIC, OF COURSE.
WE'VE BROUGHT THE BEST SOOTHSAYER IN THE LAND TO TELL US WHO IS DESTINED TO GUIDE US ALL.
WHICH MEANS THAT ANYONE COULD BE THE NEW KING.
ANY ONE OF YOU... OR EVEN ME.
THE SOOTHSAYER DEMANDS AN OFFERING IN EXCHANGE FOR ACCURACY.
THERE'S A WAY OUT AT THE BOTTOM OF THE STAIRS.
THEY'LL SEE US!
EVERYONE'S FOCUSED ON THE SPEECH, ANYWAY.
BUT THE GUARDS—
YOU'RE WITH ME, DON'T WORRY.
WE HAVE THE TRAITOROUS WYTTE PATRIARCH AND HIS WIFE.

THEY WILL SERVE AS A SACRIFICE.
NOW YOU'LL SEE WHAT HAPPENS TO THOSE WHO DARE TO CHALLENGE US!
HANS! ANGELA!
WHAT'S THIS?
WHO IS THIS JERK, HILDE?
HE DESTROYED OUR LIVING ROOM.
HE'S IN CHARGE OF THE PRISON.
ARE YOU SERIOUS?
LET'S SEE HOW FAR HE'S WILLING TO GO TO GET RID OF US.
ARE THOSE DORIAN AND DANI'S PARENTS?!
WE HAVE TO HELP THEM!
WHAT?!
YES!
LET'S GO.
WAIT!
NICO, YOU STAY HERE.
YOU'LL NEVER GET THEM OUT OF THERE.
IT'S TOO DANGEROUS.
WHAT, YOU CARE ALL OF A SUDDEN?
YOU'RE NOT MY FATHER!
LET ME GO ALREADY.
NICO—!

I SEE SOMETHING...
LET'S GO, DAMIEN.
WAIT A MINUTE, I WANT TO HEAR THIS.
BUT IT COULD BE DANGEROU—
PLEASE, WILL.
THIS IS IMPORTANT.
HAHA.
AH... OKAY.
I SEE SOMETHING...
I SEE WAR, DARKNESS...
A BLACK, DRIPPING CROWN...
I HEAR SCREAMS...
AND ROARS.
AND A NAME...
WYTTE.
WHAT...?
SO I WAS RIGHT...
OH NO.
...

CHAPTER 18

DORIAN, WAIT!
WHERE ARE THE WYTTES?! THEY'RE HERE, RIGHT?
WHAT ARE YOU PLANNING TO DO WITH THAT TOY?
SO YOU'RE THE LITTLE TRAITOR...
DORIAN, WAIT FOR ME!
DON'T TRY TO STOP ME, DANI.
ZZZZZ
WE HAVE TO FIND DAD AND MOM!
I'M NOT TRYING TO STOP YOU...
I WANT TO HELP YOU!

NOW. WHERE IS MY CROWN?
SO MASTER WAS RIGHT...
AT LEAST DORIAN AND DANI'S PARENTS AREN'T IN DANGER ANYMORE.
WEREN'T THEY TRAITORS?
BUT DO THEY WANT TO START A WAR? I'VE GOT BETTER THINGS TO DO.
WHAT ARE YOU SAYING, TRAITOR?!
WHAT CHAOS...
I THINK THAT TAKING REVENGE NOW WOULD JUST MAKE THINGS MORE COMPLICATED.
WE'VE BEEN PEACEFUL.
YOU DON'T CARE ABOUT YOUR ANCESTORS?
SAY THAT AGAIN IF YOU DARE!
WAIT. IS THAT...?
...!
WILL!
I FINALLY CAUGHT UP!
PRINCESS?

WHAT'S WRONG?
I... I SAW HIM!
HE'S IN THE MIDDLE OF THE CROWD!
IT LOOKS LIKE HE'S SAFE...
SHOULD I GO TO HIM?
MAYBE THAT WOULD MAKE THINGS WORSE... I DON'T KNOW!
IT'S BEEN SO LONG SINCE I SAW HIM!
WHO ARE YOU TALKING ABOUT?
PRINCE WILLIAM! MY FIANCÉ!
WHAT?! GO GET HIM!
BUT DORIAN AND DANI—
I CAN TAKE CARE OF DANI AND DORIAN!
ARE YOU SURE YOU CAN MAKE IT ON YOUR OWN?
OF COURSE! I'M YOUR BODYGUARD, AFTER ALL!
OKAY, SEE YOU LATER! BE CAREFUL!
GO GET HIM!
ALONE AGAIN.
HEY, DAMIEN...
WHAT ABOUT THE OTHERS?
I CAN'T CARRY ALL OF THEM AT ONCE!
I'LL COME BACK FOR THEM LATER.
HOLD ON TIGHT!
IT'S BEEN SO LONG SINCE YOU TOOK ME FOR A RIDE.
HEY, WHAT ARE YOU DOING?!
HUH...?
GERONIMOOOOOOOO
OOOOO!

WHOA!
AAAA
GRAAAAGH
YOU!
UGH...
WHAT THE HELL IS WRONG WITH YOU, AMIR?
WE COULD HAVE DIED!
AND NOW THE BROOM IS BROKEN. HOW ARE YOU GOING TO ESCAPE?
YOU HAD NO INTENTION OF COMING BACK FOR US, DID YOU?
YOU DON'T CARE ABOUT THE REST AT ALL.
THAT'S NOT—
DON'T MAKE THAT FACE, YOU'RE LIKE AN OPEN BOOK.
WHAT ARE YOU ARGUING ABOUT?
NOTHING.
C'MON, WE'VE GOT TO FIND A BROOM AND SAVE THE OTHERS
WHAT THE HECK IS GOING ON UP THERE?
ZZZZ
HERE, TAKE MY WAND!
I'VE BEEN TRYING TO GIVE IT TO YOU—
YOU'LL MAKE BETTER USE OF IT.
NO WAY, THAT WAND IS YOURS!
HOW CAN YOU DO MAGIC WITHOUT IT?

I...
I DON'T WANT TO MAKE MAGIC ANYMORE.
EVERY TIME I TRY, THINGS GO WRONG AND SOMEONE GETS HURT.
DANI, OUR HOUSE HAS BEEN DESTROYED AND OUR FAMILY ARE PRISONERS.
TODAY IT'S ALL ABOUT HURTING THEM AS MUCH AS WE CAN.
WHAT IF I END UP KILLING SOMEONE BY ACCIDENT?
LIKE THE GIANT SQUID?
DON'T BE SILLY.
JUST KEEP CASTING SPELLS!
...
OUCH!
COWARD, ATTACKING ME FROM BEHIND!
OH.
AH!

DORIAN?
THE DELINQUENT! HOW DID YOU ESCAPE?
WELL, THAT'S NOT IMPORTANT NOW...
WAIT A MINUTE!
ARE YOU REALLY ON THEIR SIDE?
...
HE WAS A PRISONER OF THE WITCHES...
IS HE REALLY MY ENEMY?
AAARGH!
I DIDN'T CHANGE SIDES. I JUST CAME HERE FOR MY PARENTS.
THANK YOU.
WHO AM I TO SAY WHETHER YOU SHOULD BE IN JAIL? I DON'T EVEN KNOW WHAT YOU DID.
ZZZZZ
YOU'RE A GOOD GUY, DORIAN.
I OWE YOU ONE!
HURRY UP!
OKAY.
WHO WAS THAT KID, WILLIAM?
WILLIAM?
IT CAN'T BE...
HE AND HIS SISTER TOOK ME TO THE JAIL!
WHAT?
HAVE YOU FOUND A BROOM?
NOT YET.

"THE WITCHES HAVE KIDNAPPED MY DEAR WILL, MY PRINCE."
IS IT...?
"PRINCES TALK AND DRESS TO PERFECTION, AND TREAT GIRLS LIKE DAMSELS."
"THEY SMELL GOOD AND KNOW HOW TO BEHAVE IN EVERY OCCASION."
"LIKE MY WILL!"
SHOULD I STOP HIM? BUT THEN...
SHE WOULD GO BACK TO THE PALACE, RIGHT?

WHERE IS MY CROWN?
WAIT A MOMENT, MY DEAR BROTHER.
HOW ARE YOU THAT SURE YOU'RE THE NEW KING?
I'M A WYTTE TOO, REMEMBER?
WELL, BECAUSE I'M THE PATRIARCH, OF COURSE.
SO WHAT?
NOBODY SAID IT HAD TO BE A MAN.
WE COULD HAVE A QUEEN INSTEAD OF A KING!
I DON'T THINK SO...
THE LOGICAL CHOICE WOULD BE FOR THE MOST POWERFUL ONE OF US TO TAKE THE THRONE.
ARE YOU IMPLYING THAT YOU'RE MORE POWERFUL THAN ME, HILDE?
I'M IMPLYING THAT I DESERVE THE CROWN!
I WAS THE ONE WHO ORGANIZED ALL OF THIS.
EXCUSE ME... I WANT TO CLARIFY SOMETHING...
FIRST, I NEED A SACRIFICE FOR MY CRYSTAL BALL,
OR IT WILL EAT ME AS PAYMENT—
THE CRYSTAL BALL CAN HAVE HIM.
WHAT?
HOLD ON!
WAIT!
NOOO! HELP ME!
AND THE SECOND THING...
I'M NOT SURE IF WE'LL HAVE A KING OR QUEEN...

BUT IT'S NOT ONE OF YOU. IT'S A CHILD.
ONE OF THE WYTTE CHILDREN.
WHAT?! THAT MAKES NO SENSE, THEY'RE JUST KIDS!
YOU MUST BE KIDDING.
HANS, HILDE, WHILE YOU'RE ARGUING, TRAITORS ARE ESCAPING.
OH... YOU'RE RIGHT, ANGELA.
WE SHOULD DO SOMETHING ABOUT THAT.
WE'LL FIND THE KIDS LATER.
YES... I THINK IT'S TIME TO RELEASE THE DRAGONS.
SO DANI AND DORIAN AREN'T HERE, EITHER...
WHERE ARE THEY?
HOW ARE YOU DOING, DANI?
FINE!
BUT I'M SCARED OF HURTING SOMEONE UNINTENTIONALLY.
DON'T BE SILLY, IT'S JUST A DEBILITATING SPELL.
WHAT'S ALL THIS?
THOSE KIDS... AREN'T THEY THE TRAITORS?
WE'RE NOT SURE ANYMORE.
DON'T YOU SEE THEY'RE ATTACKING EVERYONE?
EH...
I'LL FINISH THEM, YOU COWARDS!
HEY, YOU.
TRAITOR.
LEAVE ME ALONE!

UGH!
SHE'S INCREDIBLY POWERFUL.
THAT'S ALL?
HA.
NOT BAD.
DANI!
AH!
HAVE A TASTE OF YOUR OWN MEDICINE!
DORIAN...
DORIAN!

UGH.
A DEBILITATING SPELL...SO CHILDISH.
ARE YOU ALL RIGHT?
LET'S DO SOMETHING MORE INTERESTING...
MPH...
SAY GOODBYE TO YOUR SISTER, TRAITOR.
DORIAN!
WHAT...?
FIRE...
CARLO?
?

AH! I LOST SIGHT OF WILL...
HEY, BE CAREFUL!
EXCUSE ME...
BUT THERE ARE TOO MANY PEOPLE...
I'M IN A HURRY—
OKAY...
THAT'S ENOUGH.
POW!
GET OUT OF MY WAY!
LET ME THROUGH!
I *SAID* I'M IN A HURRY!
LET ME GO!
AGH!

WHERE IS HE?
WILL IS GONE!
WHAT NOW?
DO I GO AFTER HIM?
COME ON, MONICA,
YOU'VE DONE THIS BEFORE...
YOU CAN DO IT AGAIN!
THERE WE GO.

WHERE'S WILL?
I LOSE SIGHT OF HIM FOR A SECOND AND HE DISAPPEARS.
THEY'RE ALL CRAZY!
KILLING THE KING?!
DO THEY WANT ANOTHER WAR?
IT'S BEST TO LEAVE. NOW.
I DON'T KNOW ABOUT YOU, BUT I DON'T WANT TO BE ASSOCIATED WITH THE WYTTES...
I HAVE NOTHING AGAINST NON-MAGIC PEOPLE.
LET'S GO, BEFORE THOSE GUYS CATCH US!
DAMIEN! YOU LOOK SO HAPPY...
DO YOU LIKE WAR, AND DEATH, AND—?
OF COURSE NOT!
DID YOU FIND A BROOM?
YEAH, HERE IT IS—!
...WAS.

WHOA... IS THAT A DRAGON?
YEAH... I HEARD THEY WERE RAISING THEM.
COOL!
WILL, WHERE ARE YOU GOING?!
I WANT TO RIDE A DRAGON!
LET ME GO!
I MUST RIDE A DRAGON—
THAT'S WHAT PRINCES DO!
PLUS, WE NEED A WAY OUT OF HERE.
HAVE YOU LOST YOUR MIND?!
I'M A PRINCE, DAMN IT!
I'M NOT USELESS. TRUST ME. FOR ONCE!
NO.
...
DON'T SULK, WILL.
LET'S GO, THIS IS TOO DANGEROUS.
UH... DAMIEN...
WHAT?
DAMIEN!
I SAID WHA—

UGH.
AAAAAAH!
WILL! WHERE ARE YOU GOING?
COME BACK HERE!
NOW YOU'LL SEE...

WHAT THE...
YOU'VE GOTTA BE KIDDING!
COME ON!
STEP ASIDE, WILL.
IT'S BOUNCING OFF THE SCALES...
HEY, WATCH IT!
!
GET OFF!
H-HOW?!
TAKE MY HAND!

AHH!
SLAP
WILL!
ARE YOU ALL RIGHT, DAMIEN?
AH...
WE NEED A BROOM!
YES.
DORIAN! GET AWAY FROM THE DRAGON!
IT JUST DISINTEGRATED SOMEONE!
WHY ISN'T IT ATTACKING YOU?
AH...
IS IT...

IT *IS* YOU, ISN'T IT?
OF COURSE IT IS!
HAHA.
HE HATCHED FROM THE EGG I TRIED TO STEAL.
THE SHELL BROKE OPEN AND WE SAW EACH OTHER.
I THINK IT IMPRINTED ON ME. IT THINKS I'M ITS MOM!
REALLY? HOW CUTE!
THAT'S WHY IT'S PROTECTING ME—
AARGH!
MORE DRAGONS!
ARE THEY GOING TO FIGHT?
WE HAVE TO DO SOMETHING.
I'VE GOT AN IDEA!
SINCE OUR BROOM IS BROKEN...

COME ON, TAKE MY HAND.
A-ARE YOU SURE ABOUT THIS?
I'VE NEVER LIKED FLYING.
DON'T WORRY! YOU'RE A MASTER OF DRAGONS, DORIAN.
IT'S A CONSTANT FEELING OF INSECURITY.
THE HIGHER YOU GO, THE WORSE THE FALL.
WHOA!
TELL HIM TO TAKE US TO THE FLOATING ROCK.
HOW DO I TELL HIM THAT?!

BUT HERE I AM.
WE HAVE TO FIND MOM AND DAD!
THE DRAGONS ARE OUT OF CONTROL.
AND THE PEOPLE...
MY SPELLS JUST BOUNCE OFF...
OOPS...
DO YOU THINK WE CAN JUMP?
OF COURSE!
HEY, WAIT!

UGH!
I'M COMING, DANI...
AH!
AAH!
CRACK
CRACK
HUH?
DANI—

I'VE GOT YOU!
THE HIGHER YOU GO...
COME ON, GET ON...
YOU'VE TAMED THE DRAGON!
AMAZING—
AH!
DANI!

...THE
WORSE THE
FALL.

...
WHAT AM I SUPPOSED TO DO NOW?!

CHAPTER 20

UGH...
I'M DIZZY...
AND MY HEAD HURTS...
SO BLURRY.
BLOOD?
RIGHT...
WE FELL.
WHY DIDN'T THE DRAGON CATCH US?
WHERE *IS* THE DRAGON?
WHERE IS *DANI*?
DANI!
CAN YOU HEAR ME?
WAKE UP!
AGH!

MY LEG...
I CAN'T WALK.
OVER HERE!
I FOUND THOSE DAMN KIDS!
YOU...
YOU'RE THE ONES WHO SHOT US DOWN, RIGHT?
WHAT'S WITH ALL THIS ICE?
PUT THE WAND DOWN!
LEAVE US ALONE.
HOW DID YOU RIDE THAT DRAGON? WHO ARE YOU?
I SAID...
LEAVE US ALONE!

WHAT THE—
HE'S ATTACKING!
I WARNED YOU.
WHAT'S THIS? YOU HAVEN'T CAPTURED THEM YET?
WE GOT THE GIRL.
WE'RE HOPING SHE'S DEAD.
AH!
UGH...
DANI...
SHE CAN'T BE...
UH...

SO THAT'S WHAT YOU WANT?
TO KILL US?
THERE ARE TOO MANY OF THEM.
I NEED SOMETHING MORE POWERFUL.
MORE EFFECTIVE.
MORE VIOLENT.
THERE'S NO OTHER SOLUTION...
...RIGHT?
I CAN'T SEE WILL ANYWHERE...
I MUST FIND HIM.
WILL?
AH—

DORIAN!
THERE YOU ARE, FINALLY! I'M SO GLAD YOU'RE ALL RIGHT.
WE WERE SO WORRIED ABOUT YOU!
IS HE IGNORING ME?
NOW ISN'T THE MOMENT—
HUH?
WHO ARE THESE PEOPLE?
AND WHAT HAPPENED TO THEM?
WHAT DO I DO?
WHAT IF...

HE'S DANGEROUS?
WHAT IF IT'S HIM...
THE EVIL KING?
OF COURSE NOT. THAT'S STUPID.
DORIAN!
OUCH!
BE CAREFUL.
DORIAN, STOP THIS!
YOU'RE SCARING ME. DORIAN.
FROG KID!
WHAT IS *WRONG* WITH YOU?

HEY!
MONICA? WHAT ARE YOU DOING HERE?
WHAT ARE YOU DOING, DORIAN?
WHAT'S WRON—
SHUT UP.
I DON'T KNOW WHETHER TO HUG OR SLAP YOU RIGHT NOW.
YOU SCARED ME TO DEATH. YOU LOOKED POSSESSED.
WHAT DID YOU THINK YOU WERE DOING?
I WAS JUST DEFENDING MYSELF.
DEFENDING YOURSELF?!

FROM WHO?
I—
I DIDN'T REALIZE...
I DON'T KNOW WHAT HAPPENED.
I JUST WANTED TO DEFEND MYSELF, BUT—
HOW COULD I? I WAS THINKING ABOUT DANI—
DANI!
AH!
WHAT HAPPENED TO HER?
DANI, WAKE UP!
IS SHE...?
SHE'S UNCONSCIOUS. BUT SHE'S BLEEDING.
CAST A HEALING SPELL!

I HAVEN'T STUDIED ANY YET!
WHAT DO YOU MEAN? THAT'S THE MOST IMPORTANT THING, YOU SHOULD HAVE STUDIED HEALING FIRST!
WE NEED A DOCTOR. WHERE'S YOUR BROOM?
IT BROKE DURING THE BATTLE.
MINE TOO!
YOURS?
WE HAVE NO CHOICE.
...MONICA?
WE'LL GO ON FOOT.
WHAT?!
LET ME CARRY HER, SHE'S HEAVY.
IT'S FINE, I CAN CARRY HER. BESIDES, YOU'RE HURT.
UGH—
YOU HAVEN'T EVEN GONE A STEP AND YOU'RE OUT OF BREATH.
CAN YOU HELP ME GET HER ON MY BACK? THAT'LL BE EASIER.
WHY DID THAT VAN JUST STOP?
AH! BUT THAT'S—

THERE YOU ARE!
SEE, LITTLE GUY? WE FOUND THEM.
DANI?!
WHAT HAPPENED TO HER?
SHE HIT HER HEAD.
I'M PERFECTLY CAPABLE!
I'LL CARRY HER.
PLEASE...
LET ME BE USEFUL. FOR ONCE.
PLEASE.
I CAN CARRY YOU INSTEAD, DORIAN.
WHAT? NO WAY!
YOUR LEG IS INJURED! COME ON, I DON'T MIND.
HEY, YOU'RE BIG AGAIN!
AND WHOSE FAULT IS IT THAT I'M USUALLY TINY?
I'M FINE, SEE?
DORIAN! YOU'LL FALL!
C'MON, LITTLE PIXIE. HURRY IT UP.
I'M NOT A PIXIE!
ARGH!
POW
I TOLD YOU!

YOU'RE THE BEST HEALER, BARRY.
LET ME DRIVE.
OKAY.
WHERE SHOULD I TAKE YOU?
THE CASTLE, PLEASE!
WHAT? AREN'T WE GOING BACK HOME?
AH... BECAUSE YOU KNOW, NICO...
DON'T YOU REMEMBER WHAT THE MASTER SAID ABOUT, UM...?
OH. NOW I GET IT.
THE MASTER SAID HE MIGHT KILL DANI AND DORIAN.
ALSO, I'M SURE MY DEAR WILL IS ALREADY WAITING FOR ME THERE!
RIGHT. DIDN'T YOU SEE HIM?
YES. UNFORTUNATELY I LOST SIGHT OF HIM.
BUT HE WAS ESCAPING, SO I'M SURE HE MANAGED TO GET HOME.
HAHAHA!
MONICA, YOU NEVER CHANGE...
DANI!
YOU'RE AWAKE!

NOW THAT DANI IS SAFE, COULD YOU STOP THE VAN, PLEASE?
WHAT?!
WE CAME HERE LOOKING FOR OUR PARENTS.
THEY COULD STILL BE IN DANGER.
I MUST SAVE THEM!
COME ON, DUDE!
DO YOU THINK YOU'RE A HERO FROM A FAIRY TALE OR SOMETHING?
HEY, NICO!
AND YOU TOO!
BOTH OF YOU THINK YOU CAN SOLVE ALL THE WORLD'S PROBLEMS ALONE!
YOU ALWAYS LEAVE US BEHIND.
HEY... LEAVE HIM—
YOU LIE TO US AND YOU LEAVE DURING THE NIGHT WITH NOTHING BUT A CREEPY NOTE.
WE'RE AWARE, DORIAN, THAT YOU THINK YOU'RE POWERFUL AND UNBEATABLE.
BUT YOU KNOW WHAT?
WE GOOD-FOR-NOTHINGS HAVE SAVED YOUR LIFE TWICE!
I NEVER SAID YOU DIDN'T.
I JUST WANT TO HELP MY PARENTS.
YOU DON'T GET IT!
YOUR PARENTS ARE—
NICO!
THAT'S ENOUGH.
SO YOU CAN'T GET MAD.
WE ALL DO STUPID THINGS FOR OUR LOVED ONES.

BUT I AGREE ON ONE THING.
DORIAN, I FORBID YOU TO GO ANYWHERE.
YOU DON'T NEED TO WORRY, BECAUSE I...
I SAW YOUR PARENTS.
REALLY?
YOUR MOM IS BEAUTIFUL. SHE HAS LONG BLACK HAIR AND A BIG SCAR ON HER FACE.
AND YOUR DAD HAS SMALL EYES AND A FUNNY MUSTACHE.
THAT'S THEM ALL RIGHT.
WERE THEY ARRESTED?
NO. THEY WERE SAFE, COMPLETELY SAFE. I PROMISE!
OH, I'M SO RELIEVED.
DO YOU THINK WE'LL BE ABLE TO FIND THEM ONCE EVERYTHING SETTLES DOWN A BIT?
OF COURSE!
BUT FIRST, WE NEED TO GET YOU TWO TO A SAFE PLACE.
TRUST ME.
YES,
I... I TRUST YOU.
GOOD.
I'M STARVING!
TECHNICALLY, I DIDN'T LIE.
I'LL TELL THEM THE TRUTH ONCE WE GET OUT OF HERE.
WHOA, THIS PIZZA HAS WEIRD GREEN THINGS!
GREEN THINGS ARE HEALTHY!
DON'T LIE TO HER, ALEX.
THIS PIZZA IS FROM FOUR WEEKS AGO!

FEELING BETTER?
DEFINITELY BETTER, THANK YOU! BUT MY HEAD STILL HURTS A LITTLE.
I'VE GOT SOMETHING FOR YOU!
STAY STILL FOR A MOMENT...
HUH?!
DONE!
HOW USEFUL CAN A BAND-AID REALLY BE?
EVERY WOUND YOU GET IS PROOF OF COURAGE.
THE MORE SCARS AND BAND-AIDS YOU HAVE, THE MORE PEOPLE WILL SEE HOW STRONG YOU ARE.
COOL, HUH?
YEAH! I'M A TOUGH GIRL!
YOU DIDN'T LOOK LIKE SUCH A TOUGH GUY WHEN I FOUND YOU CRYING AT THE FLOATING ROCK, NICO.
CRYING? DON'T LIE.
IS THAT WHY YOU WEAR AN EARRING, TOO? SO PEOPLE CAN SEE THAT YOU'RE A LITTLE PUNK?
COOL, RIGHT?
ALREADY?!
UNO!

YEAH, YOU SHOULD GET MORE.
DO YOU THINK SO?
WHAT DO YOU THINK, DANI?
HMMM... DO IT IF YOU FEEL LIKE IT,
BUT YOU'RE GONNA HAVE THE SAME BABY FACE.
HEY!
HAHAHA.
YOU'RE NOT EXACTLY SCARY, NICO.
BUT TRUST ME, I'M THE MAKEOVER EXPERT!
JUST LOOK HOW GORGEOUS I MADE YOUR FRIEND LOOK.
THAT'S RIGHT, MONICA! I LOVE YOUR NEW LOOK.
STOP, YOU'RE MAKING ME BLUSH.
IF YOU WANT, WE CAN DO YOU ONCE WE ARRIVE AT THE CASTLE!
OH NO, THAT'S OKAY.
PLAY A CARD ALREADY OR I'LL BEAT YOU ONCE AND FOR ALL.
DUDE, DON'T BE A PARTY POOPER!
BEAT ME? BUT YOU HAVE SO MANY CARDS!
AND A TEN-YEAR-OLD IS BEATING YOU.
I'M TWELVE. ALMOST THIRTEEN!
HEY, DORIAN?
YEAH?

HOW DO YOU THINK I LOOK?
DO I LOOK LIKE A REAL WITCH?
DORIAN?
HUH?
WELL... I THINK YOU LOOK...
...TOO OLD.
WHAT?
THAT'S BRAVE, KID.
OH, DORIAN...
HE'LL REGRET THAT.
UNBELIEVABLE! YOU'RE SO RUDE, FROG KID!
ARE YOU CALLING ME AN "OLD WOMAN"?
YOU LOOK VERY PRETTY, OKAY?
I DON'T WANT YOU TO TEACH ME ANYMORE! YOU'RE SUCH A BOOR!
HUH? WHAT DID YOU SAY?
NOTHING.
I DIDN'T HEAR YOU. WHAT WAS IT?
I DIDN'T SAY ANYTHING.

I WON!
I DEMAND A REMATCH!
IF YOU PLAY ANOTHER ROUND, I'M IN.
COOL, LET'S ALL PLAY. I'LL CRUSH YOU ALL!
I'LL PASS.
ARE YOU JOINING US, DORIAN?
ME? SURE!
!
GUYS... THERE'S SOMEONE IN THE MIDDLE OF THE ROAD.
JUST DODGE THEM.
THERE ISN'T ENOUGH SPACE.
HONK HONK
THEY'RE NOT MOVING!
THEY'RE ATTACKING US!
AAAAAAAH!

TELL ME...
WHERE ARE THE KIDS?
MARK!
HEY, MARK!
YAWN
HE'S SO GROGGY!
WE'RE IN TROUBLE! MARK?!
EVANS
HERE HE COMES! HE'S SO HANDSOME...
WAIT... WHAT THE—
AAAAAAAH!
OH NO! THE DOUGHNUT!
KLANK
EXCUSE ME.
NICO!
I KNEW IT!
I'VE BEEN YELLING FOR HALF AN HOUR.
WHAT HAPPENED TO YOU?!

YOU'RE—
DON'T YOU DARE MAKE FUN OF ME!
AND JUST TO BE CLEAR, YOU'RE STILL MY ARCHENEMY!
I'M ONLY HERE BECAUSE I HAVE NO OTHER CHOICE!
BUT WHAT—
THE MASTER HAS LOST IT.
COME, QUICK!
IT HAPPENED EARLY THIS MORNING...
IT WASN'T NECESSARY TO STEAL THEIR VAN, MASTER!
I COULDN'T CARRY ALL OF YOU. THEY'LL BE OKAY.
WHAT ARE YOU PLANNING TO DO WITH DANI AND DORIAN?
THEY'LL REMAIN LOCKED IN HERE FOR NOW.
AND THEN WHAT?
YOU'LL KILL THEM?
THEY'RE INNOCENT! THEY HAVE NO IDEA ABOUT ANY OF IT!
I KNOW.
THAT'S WHY I MUST CONSULT THE CRYSTAL BALL FIRST.
BUT WE DON'T HAVE MANY OPTIONS.
EVEN IF THEY STILL DON'T KNOW,
ONE OF THEM IS GOING TO TURN EVIL SOONER OR LATER. THAT'S A FACT.

I DON'T CARE WHAT YOU SAY! YOU WON'T HURT THEM!
MASTER, LET US TALK WITH THEM.
...
SEE YOU LATER.
WHAT A MESS.
DON'T WORRY, NICO. WE'LL PROTECT THEM!
NOTHING CAN HAPPEN WHILE WE'RE STANDING HERE.
BUT AS SOON AS THE SUN COMES UP, I'LL BE SMALL AGAIN.
THAT'S RIGHT. YOU SHOULD GO GET HELP!
YEAH... I'LL GO BEFORE MASTER COMES BACK.
OKAY. I'LL STAY AND KEEP WATCH ON MY ROOM.
DOES IT BOTHER YOU THAT THEY'RE IN YOUR ROOM?
OF COURSE! IT'S MY PRIVATE SPACE!
MY DIARY IS IN THERE! WHAT IF DORIAN READS IT?!
DON'T BE STUPID!
HE WOULDN'T DO THAT.
DORIAN'S STILL A LITTLE KID. HE ISN'T INTERESTED IN WHAT GIRLS THINK ABOUT.
ALL HE THINKS ABOUT ARE HIS BOOKS AND HIS STUPID FROG. YOU CAN RELAX.
HAHA... RIGHT. I WAS BEING SILLY.
I'LL BE BACK SOON WITH REINFORCEMENTS.

UGH...
DANI!
WHERE ARE WE?
WE'RE IN MONICA'S ROOM, BUT I DON'T KNOW HO—
WHAT ARE YOU DOING?! YOU'RE NOT GOING IN THERE!
YOU CAN'T DO THIS, MASTER!
PRINCESS...
PRINCESS, I MUST. I HAVE NO OTHER OPTION.
WHAT DO YOU MEAN, NO OTHER OPTION?! YOU'RE GOING TO KILL THEM?!
BUT THEY HAVEN'T DONE ANYTHING WRONG!
...
I DON'T WANT TO FIGHT WITH YOU.
YOU CAN'T BE SERIOUS.
IF YOU HAD SEEN THE HORRIFYING THINGS I SAW IN THE CRYSTAL BALL, YOU WOULDN'T HESITATE, EITHER...
YOU HEARD THAT SOOTHSAYER AT THE SABBATH. YOU KNOW YOUR FATHER IS THEIR FIRST TARGET—
POW
AGH!
HUH?
WHAT THE—

EVANS!
I CAN'T BELIEVE MY EYES, PENDRAGON...
NICO, YOU TRAITOR!
KILLING KIDS? SERIOUSLY? I DON'T RECOGNIZE YOU.
TRAITOR?! AT LEAST HE HAS SOME SENSE!
CAN I GO IN TOO?
YOU DON'T UNDERSTAND ANYTHING, EVANS!
THEN TRY TO EXPLAIN IT TO ME SO I DON'T HAVE TO HIT YOU AGAIN!
DORIAN...
DANI...
YOU'RE AWAKE.
...
...
DANI...
I MUST... KILL...
HUUH?!
DANG, I FORGOT ABOUT THAT LITTLE PROBLEM...!
PLEASE DON'T KILL ME!
I'M SORRY...
SO THAT HAPPENS SOMETIMES... I'M FINE NOW.
ARE YOU SURE?
WHAT WAS ALL THAT ABOUT?
MONICA.
I...
WHAT ARE YOU HIDING FROM US?

...
WHY ARE WE IN HERE?
WHAT'S GOING ON?
...
OKAY.
BUT I RECOMMEND YOU SIT DOWN.
THIS WON'T BE EASY TO HEAR.
...AND THAT'S WHY THE MASTER DECIDED TO LOCK YOU IN.
WHAT ARE WE SUPPOSED TO DO NOW?
I CAN'T BELIEVE IT...
A WITCH REBELLION?! AND THEY WANT TO GET RID OF EVERYONE WHO DOESN'T USE MAGIC?
BUT THAT'S INSANE!
THAT'S WHAT IT LOOKS LIKE...
ALL THIS TIME...
DAD AND MOM HAVE BEEN THE BAD ONES. AND AUNT HILDE TOO.
AND WE DIDN'T REALIZE...
AND THAT NEW KING OF THE WITCHES...
IT MAKES SENSE...
WE WON'T BE ABLE TO STOP IT.

WAIT. WHAT?
WHAT DO YOU MEAN, YOU WON'T BE ABLE TO STOP IT?
THE WYTTE SON.
A POWERFUL YOUNG PERSON TO GUIDE THE NEXT GENERATION OF WITCHES IN A NEW WAR...
IT'S POSSIBLE. PROBABLE, EVEN.
?
WHAT ARE YOU SAYING, DORIAN?
HUH?
I'VE RISKED MY NECK TO PROTECT YOU!
I STOPPED THE MASTER FROM HURTING YOU BECAUSE I TRUSTED YOU!
AND NOW YOU'RE TELLING ME THAT THE MASTER WAS RIGHT?!
SHOULD I HAVE LET HIM KILL YOU?!
YOU'RE PLANNING TO KILL MY FATHER?! YOU'RE PLANNING TO KILL ME?!
HUH?
DO YOU THINK I'M TALKING ABOUT MYSELF?
DO YOU REALLY THINK WE WOULD DO SOMETHING LIKE THAT?
IF NOT YOU, WHO?
A WYTTE SON. WITH YOUR FACE? THE PROPHECY WAS CLEAR.
YES. THERE IS SOMEONE WHO FITS THAT DESCRIPTION.
WE NEVER TALK ABOUT HIM BECAUSE WE'RE NOT PROUD TO BE RELATED TO HIM.

ACTUALLY, IT'S BEEN A LONG TIME SINCE WE SAW HIM. YEARS.
ALL WE KNOW IS THAT HE'S TERRIFYING.
YES.
AND MEAN.
HE'S POWERFUL AND HE DOESN'T LISTEN TO REASON.
SO THE NEW KING OF THE WITCHES IS...
OUR BIG BROTHER.
DAMIEN.
IT MUST BE HIM.
IS THAT...
A GOOD THING?
YES! NOW WE JUST HAVE TO DEFEAT THEIR EVIL BROTHER!
DAMIEN? I KNOW A DAMIEN...
AH!
WYTTE...
OF COURSE, THAT'S WHY THE NAME WYTTE SOUNDED SO FAMILIAR!
DAMIEN WYTTE!
I KNOW HIM!
HE LIVES IN THE CASTLE!

SO, DAMIEN IS YOUR BROTHER...
I'M LOST.
HE'S BEEN LIVING AT THE CASTLE?
DO YOU KNOW HIM?!
DO YOU THINK HE COULD FIT THE MASTER'S PROPHECY?
DOES HE LOOK LIKE THESE TWO?
WELL...
YES. OF COURSE. THEY'RE SIBLINGS, AFTER ALL.
YOU'RE NOT DANGEROUS, THEN?
LIKE I SAID.
NO, BUT... WHAT DO WE DO NOW?
GOOD QUESTION, DANI.
THIS DOESN'T CHANGE ANYTHING. YOUR FAMILY IS STILL EVIL.
MASTER—
TELL ME.
IF THERE WAS A WAR,
WHOSE SIDE WOULD YOU BE ON?
NEITHER SIDE! WE DON'T WANT ANY KIND OF WAR.
WE JUST WANT EVERYONE TO GET ALONG WELL! THE ONES WHO DO MAGIC AND THE ONES WHO DON'T.
WELL, I WANTED THE SAME THING.
BUT IT'S TOO LATE NOW.

I'M GOING TO SPEAK TO THE KING.
I FORBID YOU TO LEAVE—
IT WOULD BE TERRIBLE IF YOUR PARENTS FOUND YOU.
DON'T LISTEN TO HIM. HE WOULDN'T HURT A FLY.
...
HE'S JUST CONFUSED... ANYWAY, IT'S ALREADY TEN IN THE MORNING. TIME TO GO BACK TO WORK, MARK.
AHH!!
YES, DAD.
THANK YOU SO MUCH FOR HELPING US, MARK!
BEFORE YOU GO, CAN I TALK TO YOU ABOUT SOMETHING?
?
SURE, GO FOR IT.
NO, I MEAN...
...JUST THE TWO OF US.
OOOOH!
WHAT IF HE TRIES TO KILL YOU?
YOU MUST BE KIDDING!
LET'S MEET TOMORROW THEN, MARK.
SURE, SEE YOU TOMORROW!

IT'S ABOUT TIME, OUR BELOVED HERO!
NICO?
SINCE YOU'RE HERE...
...I WANT TO TALK TO YOU.
I THOUGHT YOU WERE AVOIDING ME BECAUSE YOU WERE STILL MAD...
BUT I GUESS I WAS WRONG.
WHAT HAPPENED? WHO SHRANK YOU?
ASK YOUR GIRLFRIEND.
WHAT GIRLFRIEND?
HOW CAN YOU BE SO DENSE? I MEAN DANI, OF COURSE.
SHE WAS THE ONE WHO SHRANK ME. IT WAS A PUNISHMENT.
BECAUSE, AS YOU KNOW, I'M A JERK. I DESERVED IT.
YOU'RE NOT A JERK.
YOU'RE A GOOD PERSON, NICO.
OF COURSE I AM! AND WHAT DO YOU KNOW?!
YOU'RE MR. PERFECT WHO CAN DO ANYTHING AND KNOWS EVERYTHING!
THE ONE THAT ALWAYS COMES TO THE RESCUE!
BUT NICO—
GO AWAY AND MAKE SOME NEW FRIENDS, MARK!
HEY, NICO, WAIT!

CHAPTER 22

IT WAS PRETTY EXCITING, RIGHT, CARLO?
WHEN WE GET THE CHANCE, WE'LL GO FIND THE DRAGON.
BUT DON'T YOU WORRY, YOU'RE STILL MY BEST FRIEND.
FINISH YOUR BREAKFAST AND WE CAN GET SOME SLEEP.
UH, DORIAN?
AGH! MONICA!
WHAT ARE YOU DOING HERE?!
YOU TWO ARE SO CUTE.
I DIDN'T MEAN TO INTERRUPT YOU.
I JUST... I'M SORRY ABOUT EARLIER.
THE MASTER TOLD US HORRIBLE THINGS AND I WAS STRESSED, BUT I SHOULDN'T HAVE YELLED AT YOU.
I...
I PROMISE YOU, I'LL NEVER DOUBT YOU AGAIN!
PLEASE DON'T HATE ME. AGAIN.
ARE YOU APOLOGIZING?
YES, I AM.
IS IT THAT WEIRD?
HEY.
OF COURSE I'M NOT MAD AT YOU, MONICA.
YOU CAME LOOKING FOR US DESPITE THE DANGER.

YOU SAVED ME.
YOU'RE MY HEROINE.
ARE YOU SERIOUS?
YOUR HEROINE?!
OF COURSE!
OH... WELL... RIGHT! OF COURSE!
SO WE CAN KEEP BEING A TEAM.
YES.
SLEEP WELL, DORIAN!
SEE YOU TOMORROW.
AND... WHAT I SAID BEFORE IS STILL TRUE.
I WON'T EVER DOUBT YOU AGAIN.
WE HAVE TO TRUST EACH OTHER TO BE A TEAM!
RIGHT!

"TRUST EACH OTHER."
YEAH, RIGHT.
I LIED TO HIM.
I LIED TO EVERYONE.
THE PROPHECY—
IT WAS SOMEONE VERY YOUNG.
WITH DARK HAIR AND EYES.
WHAT ELSE COULD I HAVE DONE?
DAMIEN.
I'M SURE THE PROPHECY IS ABOUT HIM.
ANGELA, PLEASE! DAMIEN HATES US.
HE WANTS NOTHING TO DO WITH US.
I KNOW HOW TO CONVINCE HIM.
AND HOW TO CONVINCE ALL THE DESERTERS, TOO.
HOW?
WE'RE GOING TO MAKE THEM HATE THE NON-MAGICAL PEOPLE AGAIN.

CHAPTER 23

SO YOU DIDN'T SEE MY DAUGHTER?
NO, YOUR MAJESTY...
I'M SORRY.
DON'T BE. I'M RELIEVED THAT MONICA WASN'T INSIDE DURING THAT CHAOS.
I DID SEE PRINCE WILLIAM.
BUT...
I WASN'T ABLE TO RESCUE HIM.
I HAVE NO IDEA WHERE HE WENT.
BUT YOU BRING GOOD NEWS, TOO.
MOST OF THE WITCHES DECIDED NOT TO BETRAY ME.
HUH?
SOME EVEN FOUGHT TO DEFEND ME.
THAT'S TRUE.
ANYWAY, I HAVE A PLAN. IT'S RISKY, BUT...
MAYBE WE DON'T HAVE TO FIGHT.

DON'T HAVE TO FIGHT?
I'M SORRY, YOUR MAJESTY.
BUT YOU'RE BEING NAÏVE.

GOOD MORNING, EVERYONE!
GOOD MOR—
WHOA!
TA-DAA!
HOW DO I LOOK?
YOU LOOK ADORABLE, DANI.
HEY. TH-THOSE OVERALLS ARE MINE.
REALLY?
I FOUND THEM IN A BOX IN THE ATTIC.
I DON'T OWN ANY NON-BLACK CLOTHES, SO...
SORRY, I'LL RETURN THEM TO YOU RIGHT AWAY—
KEEP THEM. THEY LOOK MUCH BETTER ON YOU!
DON'T YOU WORRY, I'LL TAKE YOU SHOPPING.
SHORT HAIR REALLY LOOKS GOOD ON YOU.
I THOUGHT IT'D BE MORE COMFORTABLE THIS WAY.

WHAT DO YOU THINK, DORIAN?
IT'S HORRIBLE.
DON'T BE RUDE, DORIAN!
WHAT ARE YOU TALKING ABOUT, DORIAN?
OF COURSE WE LOOK LIKE TWINS. WE HAVE THE SAME FACE.
I DON'T GET IT.
WHY CHANGE YOUR LOOK ALL OF A SUDDEN?
WE DON'T EVEN LOOK LIKE TWINS ANYMORE.
BUT WHY DON'T YOU WANT TO WEAR BLACK?
WITCHES ARE SUPPOSED TO WEAR BLACK.
DAD WOULDN'T LIKE IT.
DAD IS PROBABLY A MURDERER.
BESIDES, I...
I WANT TO STOP BEING A WITCH.
WHAT?
I'M NOT GOOD AT THIS MAGIC THING.
I'D RATHER BE A NORMAL PERSON.
WHAT DO YOU MEAN, *NOT GOOD AT MAGIC?*

YOU WERE FIGHTING NEXT TO ME AT THE FLOATING ROCK!
YOU DEFEATED EVERYONE.
AND I KILLED A DRAGON!
I ALSO KILLED THE GIANT SQUID.
I DESTROYED MARK'S COFFEE SHOP,
MY POTION MADE HIM WANT TO KILL ME, AND...
I SHRANK NICO!
EVERY TIME I USE MAGIC, EVERYTHING ENDS UP GOING WRONG!
YOU SEE.
YOU HAVE A DUD FOR A SISTER.
I'M NOT LEAVING YOU BEHIND. JUST THE MAGIC.
YEAH, SURE!
YOU'RE A COWARD, DANI!
DORIAN—
WELL...
I'M OFF TO WORK. CAN'T BE LATE.
SEE YOU!
?
?
?
?

SO?
HOW DO I LOOK?
SOMETHING IS DIFFERENT...
I CUT MY HAIR!
YOU DIDN'T NOTICE?
WELL, NOW THAT YOU MENTION IT...
WHEN YOU ASKED ME FOR A JOB YESTERDAY, I DIDN'T THINK YOU WERE SERIOUS.
OF COURSE I'M SERIOUS. I'M READY TO WORK!
YOU'LL SEE HOW BORING NORMAL LIFE IS.
ARE YOU BORED, MARK?
ALWAYS.
EXCEPT WHEN I'M WITH YOU.
!
I MEAN, *ALL* OF YOU!
WITH YOUR BROTHER TOO, AND NICO, THE MASTER...
IT WAS MY MAGIC THAT WAS ALWAYS WRECKING THINGS.
WELL, FROM NOW ON, I'LL BE HERE. WORK WILL BE FUN!
I'M SURE I'LL BE GREAT.

SO...
MAGIC WRECKED THINGS, HUH?
MAYBE I'M A BIT CLUMSY.
HEHE.
ARE YOU SERIOUS? JUST A BIT CLUMSY?!
LUCKILY, MY DAD ISN'T HERE.
YOU CAN FIX EVERYTHING WITH MAGIC BEFORE HE COMES BACK.
I CAN'T, MARK, I TOLD YOU!
I WON'T DO MAGIC ANYMORE. EVER.
NEVER AGAIN, FOR REAL?
I WANT TO BE ABLE TO DO THINGS ON MY OWN.
AND YOU'RE THE MOST NORMAL PERSON I KNOW, SO SHOW ME HOW TO BE NORMAL!
UH... THANKS, I THINK?
I'LL TEACH YOU ABOUT LIFE WITHOUT MAGIC.
OOOH!
BUT I'M WARNING YOU. IT'LL BE ROUGH.
YOU'LL HAVE TO GET UP AT 7 AM TOMORROW. START EARLIER.
SURE!

TODAY'S THE DAY I LEARN TO BE AN ORDINARY PERSON.
7 AM
8 AM
NO SPELLS.
NO CURSES.
9 AM
NO UNDOING MISTAKES.
11 AM
1 PM

NO POTIONS.
2 PM
3 PM
NO FLYING BROOMS.
NO QUICK FIXES.
4 PM
6 PM
IN A NUTSHELL: NO MAGIC.
8 PM
...
HOW ARE YOU DOING, DANI? TIRED?
SO TIRED. THIS IS HARDER THAN I EXPECTED.
DON'T YOU WANT TO STOP SWEEPING AND GO BACK TO FLYING BROOMS?
WHAT? NO!

MARK WAS BEING KIND OF WEIRD TODAY.
I WONDER WHY...
BUT STILL, IT WAS SO FUN TO WORK IN THE CAFÉ.
FROM NOW ON, EVERY DAY WILL BE LIKE THIS.
MM?
OH...
MY BROOM...
WOULD IT BE SO BAD IF I...
JUST FOR A LITTLE WHILE?
BUT..
I MADE MYSELF A PROMISE!

A LIFE WITHOUT FLYING BROOMS.
I HOPE DORIAN IS STILL AWAKE.
OH.
OH.
D-DORIAN? WHAT ARE YOU DOING?
WAITING FOR YOU.
HOW WAS WORK? HORRIBLE?
DID YOU GET BORED?
ARE YOU EXHAUSTED?
IT WAS COOL!
I WAS A LITTLE CLUMSY, BUT I'LL TRY HARDER ON MONDAY.
SO YOU'RE GOING TO KEEP WORKING THERE?
YES.
LOOK, I'VE MADE US HOT CHOCOLATE...
IF YOU WANT, I CAN TELL YOU ALL ABOUT WORK WHILE WE DRINK IT?
NO THANKS. NIGHT.
OH... GOOD NIGHT.
...
IT DIDN'T WORK.
SHE KEEPS INSISTING ON NOT DOING MAGIC.

I DID EVERYTHING I COULD.
WE HAVE TO KEEP TRYING.
WE'LL CREATE MORE OBSTACLES. MAKE IT REALLY STRESSFUL.
DORIAN, GIVE HER SOME TIME.
IN THE END, SHE'LL REALIZE ON HER OWN.
MAGIC IS PRETTY GREAT.
I HOPE SO.

NOW GO TO THE FITTING ROOM, I WANT TO SEE YOU IN THE DRESS I CHOSE.
DORIAN IS STILL IN A BAD MOOD.
TELL ME ABOUT IT. HE'S BEEN IGNORING ME FOR DAYS.
WHAT ABOUT MAKING MY OWN DECISIONS?
I DON'T WANT HIM TO BE MAD AT ME...
DO YOU THINK I SHOULD APOLOGIZE?
NO!
YOU'RE ALLOWED TO MAKE YOUR OWN DECISIONS!
DON'T LET YOURSELF BE BULLIED!

I'M SORRY, MONICA, BUT THIS ISN'T VERY PRACTICAL.
BESIDES, I DON'T FEEL LIKE MYSELF.
BUT WHAT ARE YOU TALKING ABOUT?
YOU LOOK SUPER DUPER ADORABLE!
TRY ON THIS OTHER ONE.
THIS ONE IS EVEN WORSE...
AAAH!
I'M GOING TO DIE FROM CUTENESS OVERLOAD!
ENOUGH.
I'M CHOOSING NOW!
HEHE.
MUCH BETTER.
APPROVED.

SHOPPING IS EXHAUSTING.
WHAT ARE YOU SAYING? IT'S SO MUCH FUN!
AND YOU CAN'T WEAR NICO'S CLOTHES FOREVER.
HE DOESN'T MIND.
HUH, THAT'S ONE OF MY FATHER'S SOLDIERS.
LOOKS LIKE HE PUT UP A FLYER.
LET'S TAKE A LOOK!
COURT CIRCULAR
GREAT BALL AT THE PALACE
Next week the King is going to celebrate a great party at the palace, which THE WHOLE KINGDOM is invited to attend.
Nobles and plebeians. Peasants, craftsmen, businessmen, and witches.
A BALL?
A BALL!
NOW WE HAVE AN EXCUSE TO GO SHOPPING AGAIN!
HA HA! YES, BUT...
DOESN'T THIS SEEM A LITTLE FISHY?

CHAPTER 24

ATTENTION, PLEASE!
Ground Rules for a Party at the Palace:
I- Code of conduct towards the King
II- Code of conduct towards the guests
III- Co... conduct towards the servants
V- Dress code
V- Table manners
VI- Ball
VII- Further details
THIS WEEK I WILL BE GIVING INTENSIVE ETIQUETTE CLASSES.
SO EVERYONE KNOWS HOW TO BEHAVE AT THE BALL.
I'M ALREADY AN EXPERT.
I'VE READ MANY BOOKS ON—
LISTEN UP!
UGH.
TEACH ME HOW TO ACT RICH, PRINCESS!
OH, NICO... THE NIGHT OF THE BALL ISN'T A FULL OR NEW MOON.
CAN'T YOU BRING ME ANYWAY?
BRINGING A CURSED BOY TO THE PALACE ISN'T A GOOD IDEA.
ARE YOU SERIOUS?
YEAH, UNLESS... DANI?
SORRY, NICO. I STILL DON'T KNOW HOW TO BREAK YOUR CURSE.
LOOK ON THE BRIGHT SIDE, DANI. WITH FOUR OF US, IT'LL BE EASIER TO CHOOSE DANCE PARTNERS!
DANCE PARTNERS?
OF COURSE!
DON'T WORRY, I'VE ALREADY ARRANGED FOR YOU TO DANCE WITH MARK.
BUT WHO WILL YOU GO WITH?

WITH THAT GRUMPY LITTLE BROTHER OF YOURS. THERE'S NO OTHER OPTION.
WHAT? WITH DORIAN?
REALLY?
I'M DOING IT FOR YOU, AS A FAVOR!
THERE'S NO NEED.
I'LL GO WITH DORIAN.
WHAT? WHERE?
WHAT A RELIEF...
TO THE BALL, DORIAN! PAY ATTENTION.
BUT THEN... WHO WILL I GO WITH?
YOU'D BETTER NOT MAKE ME LOOK LIKE A FOOL, MUFFIN BOY.
HEY, I'M NOT EXACTLY THRILLED, EITHER.
WELL, I THINK YOU'LL MAKE A VERY ELEGANT COUPLE!
I AGREE, PRINCESS, HE DOESN'T DESERVE TO DANCE WITH YOU.
WELL, ARE YOU READY?
I GUESS...

LET'S GET STARTED!
DON'T STARE AT THE GROUND, IT ISN'T PROPER.
IT'S BETTER THAN FALLING ON MY FACE!
ONE, TWO, THREE...
UH...
FOLLOW THE RHYTHM!
GOOD SPIN!
AAAAAAARGH!
!
YOU'RE A MONSTER!
I'M SORRY, IT WAS AN ACCIDENT.
HAHAHA! HOW CAN YOU BE THIS USELESS, MARK?
PRACTICE WITH THE BROOM!
WHAT AM I SUPPOSED TO DO WITH IT?
PRETEND IT'S A PERSON.
AGH!
UGH!
WHOAAA!
I'M ALSO PRACTICING... I STEPPED ON MONICA'S FEET, TOO.
OH, I SEE.

YOU'RE BOTH AS BAD AS WILL.
HE STEPS ON MY FEET EVERY TIME WE DANCE.
LUCKILY...
DORIAN IS HERE.
WILL YOU DANCE WITH ME?
YOU WON'T STEP ON MY FEET, RIGHT? SINCE YOU'RE AN EXPERT?
OF COURSE NOT...
I JUST...
DON'T FEEL LIKE IT RIGHT NOW.
I KNEW IT!
YOU CAN'T DANCE, CAN YOU?
OF COURSE I CAN DANCE!
COME ON, ADMIT IT!
I'M TELLING YOU, I CAN!
I'D BE DELIGHTED TO TEACH YOU, DORIAN.
THERE'S NO NEED FOR YOU TO TEACH ME ANYTHING!
WHY CAN'T YOU JUST ADMIT YOU DON'T KNOW EVERYTHING?
HE CAN'T DANCE.
DEFINITELY CAN'T.
CAN'T DANCE AT ALL.

THIS IS HOPELESS.
MARK?!
WHAT ARE YOU DOING?
I'M SORRY, BUT IT'S IMPOSSIBLE.
I HAVE ERRANDS TO RUN.
JUST GO, YOU WON'T BE MISSED.
YOU COMING, DANI?
OF COURSE, SHE NEEDS TO MEET HER WORK OBLIGATIONS!
UM...
ALL RIGHT, I'LL COME.
IT LOOKS LIKE IT'S JUST YOU AND ME AFTER ALL, PRINCESS.
YOU CAN GIVE ME ETIQUETTE CLASSES!
MAYBE LATER.
I NEED TO SPEAK TO DORIAN.
WHAT?
SERIOUSLY?

I'M SORRY TO INTRUDE.
AAGH!
I'M HERE TO ASK YOU TO TEACH ME SOME MAGIC.
I'M NOT IN THE MOOD, MONICA.
Waltz for Beginners
YOU PROMISED! YOU DON'T WANT TO BREAK YOUR PROMISE, DO YOU?
I JUST...
CAN'T STOP THINKING ABOUT MY PARENTS. AND DANI ON TOP OF THAT. I DON'T KNOW WHAT TO DO TO MAKE THINGS RIGHT.
Basic Magic Potions Vol.1
I KNOW YOU'RE WORRIED, DORIAN. BUT AT THE END OF THE DAY, IT'S HER CHOICE.
SHE DIDN'T QUIT MAGIC BECAUSE SHE WANTED TO.
SHE DID IT BECAUSE SHE DOESN'T THINK SHE'S GOOD ENOUGH.
BUT BEING UPSET WON'T CHANGE HER MIND.
I CAN'T PRETEND TO BE HAPPY WHEN I'M NOT. THAT'S NOT WHO I AM.
YOU'RE TOO PROUD, DID YOU KNOW THAT?
PROFESSOR WYTTE...
LOOK!
THAT'S CHEATING!
MY NOTES FROM MASTER'S CLASSES ARE ALL COLOR CODED ACCORDING TO THE TYPE OF MAGIC AND LEVEL OF DIFFICULTY.
IT WOULD BE A SHAME TO TURN AWAY SUCH A METICULOUS, RIGOROUS, AND ORGANIZED STUDENT.
YOU KNOW M WEAKNESS.

I DON'T KNOW WHY I'M SPYING ON THESE TWO ALL DAY.
THE TRUTH IS...
I COULDN'T CARE LESS WHAT THEY DO.
I'M OUT.
I DON'T KNOW IF STUDYING ON THE BALCONY IS SUCH A GOOD IDEA...
YOU READ BOOKS?
OF COURSE!
BACK WHEN I LIVED AT THE PALACE, I USED TO READ IN THE GARDEN ON LOVELY DAYS LIKE THIS ONE.
I LOVE ROMANTIC STORIES WHERE YOUNG LOVERS MUST OVERCOME MANY OBSTACLES TO BE TOGETHER.
FIGHTING DRAGONS, SPIRITS, WITCHES, EVIL STEPMOTHERS...
AND THE BEST PART: THE KISS OF TRUE LOVE THAT AWAKENS THE PRINCESS FROM HER DEEP SLEEP!
AH. THAT MAKES SENSE, ACTUALLY.
KISSING SOMEONE WHO'S SLEEPING?
CREEPY.

YOU REAL-LIFE WITCHES ARE WAY MORE BORING.
IT'S A SHAME THOSE SORTS OF STORIES AREN'T REAL.
WHAT ARE YOU TALKING ABOUT?
OF COURSE THEY'RE REAL.
REALLY?
FOR INSTANCE, SOME SPELLS CAN ONLY BE BROKEN WITH CONCRETE ACTIONS,
NOT ONLY WITH A KISS, BUT BY KEEPING A PROMISE OR GETTING REVENGE...
WE CALL THEM CURSES.
WE CAN STUDY THEM, IF YOU LIKE.
I CAN TEACH YOU HOW TO CURSE PEOPLE—
NO, THANKS.
THINK ABOUT IT. CURSES ARE VERY POWERFUL.
I DON'T WANT TO.
ARE YOU SURE?
YES! NOW STOP TRYING TO SCARE ME, IT'S NOT WORKING!
HAHA! DIDN'T YOU SAY WITCHES WERE BORING?
WHAT DO YOU WANT TO STUDY, THEN?
I WANT TO LEARN HOW TO HEAL.
WHEN DANI WAS IN TROUBLE, WE WERE LUCKY TO FIND HELP.
NEXT TIME, WE SHOULD KNOW HOW TO HEAL WOUNDS OURSELVES.
HOW ABOUT A HEALING POTION?
PERFECT!
OKAY, FOR THE EASIEST ONE WE'LL NEED—
WAIT A MINUTE!
I NEED TO GET INTO THE MOOD FIRST.
?

WHAT DO YOU THINK?
IT'S THE HAT I USED ON THE FLOATING ROCK. I ADDED SOME FLOWERS.
NOW I LOOK LIKE A REAL WITCH!
MY WAY, OF COURSE.
DORIAN! YOU DON'T LIKE IT?
THERE'S SOMETHING MISSING.
?
?
?
CLOSE YOUR EYES.
WHY?
HA HA HA!
WHY NOT?
LOOK.
I JUST MEANT THIS.
YES.
IT'S A FEATHER FROM THAT SILLY BIRD, ISN'T IT?
I TOLD YOU THE BIRD WAS SIMILAR TO YOU, REMEMBER?
YEAH...
I'M HAPPY I KEPT IT.
IT LOOKS LIKE IT WAS MADE FOR YOU.

CHAPTER 25

BUT... BUT THAT BIRD WAS SO ANNOYING! IT SANG HORRIBLY.
HA HA! THAT'S TRUE!
WHAT ARE YOU TRYING TO SAY?
WELL, IT WAS ALSO VERY CUTE, SO—
!
SO...?
EH?
SERIOUSLY, I'M SICK OF THOSE TWO!
HOW CAN THEY CALL THAT WORK? THEY BASICALLY FOOL AROUND ALL DAY.
I WON'T BE LEFT OUT.
AHEM...
WE WERE JUST ABOUT TO START A POTION CLASS.
DO YOU WANT TO JOIN?
HELLO! ANYBODY HOME?
IS NICO THERE?
OH, HELLO!
HELLOOO!
WE RANG THE BELL, BUT NOBODY ANSWERED!

THOSE ARE MY FRIENDS.
ARE YOU LOOKING FOR NICO?
YEAH, CLASSES STARTED A MONTH AGO AND HE HASN'T SHOWN UP.
OH, NICO... SO YOU WERE PLAYING HOOKY?
I CAN'T GO TO CLASS LIKE THIS.
DON'T TELL THEM I'M HERE!
NICO ISN'T HOME RIGHT NOW...
BUT HE'S FINE, DON'T WORRY!
THEN, DO YOU TWO WANT TO HANG OUT?
WHAT?!
WE FOUND SOME REALLY COOL BEANS IN THE WOODS. THEY GROW STALKS THAT REACH THE SKY—
YES, OF COURSE I'LL COME!
HUH?
THEY'RE MY FRIENDS, NOT YOURS!
COME ON, MONICA! WE CAN LOOK FOR POTION INGREDIENTS IN THE WOODS.
NO, I'D BETTER STAY...
YOU KNOW I DON'T LIKE ALL THE MUD AND BUGS IN THE WOODS.

EW, YOU'RE RIGHT.
BUT I MATURED, SO THOSE THINGS DON'T BOTHER ME ANYMORE!
I HOPE.
WHAT A JOKE.
SEE YOU LATER!
...
BAH, DORIAN'S SUCH A LOSER. MY FRIENDS WILL NEVER LIKE HIM, ANYWAY.
YOU AGREE WITH ME, RIGHT?
EH?
ME? I THINK...
WELL...
HE'S...
OH NO!
I-I THINK HE'S CUTE.
WHAT?!
I MUST BE CONFUSED!
I NEED TO THINK.
ONCE AGAIN...
...THEY'VE ALL PUSHED ME AWAY.
AS IF I DIDN'T EXIST.

WELL, I DON'T CARE ABOUT THEM.
I'LL DEAL WITH THINGS BY MYSELF. I DON'T NEED ANYONE.
THE MASTER HAS BEEN GONE FOR ALMOST A WEEK NOW...
NO.
WHO CARES.
THE MASTER LEFT ME, TOO.
HE NEVER CARED ABOUT ME.
IT DOESN'T MATTER.
AND IT'S ALL BECAUSE OF—
HEY, DANI...
WHEN ARE YOU GOING TO RESTORE MY ORIGINAL SIZE?
YOU PROMISED.

I KNOW. AND I'LL DO IT, NICO, DON'T WORRY.
BUT YOU'LL NEED TO WAIT A BI—
DON'T YOU THINK I'VE WAITED LONG ENOUGH?
DO YOU THINK IT'S FUNNY?
YOU'RE SO SELFISH, DANI!
I'M NOT READY!
WHO AM I KIDDING?
I'M AFRAID TO HURT YOU,
OR EVEN KILL YOU BY ACCIDENT.
OF COURSE I CARE.
BUT IT'S TOO LATE.
COME BACK, IT'S GETTING DARK!
WHERE ARE YOU GOING?
BECAUSE AT THE END OF THE DAY, IT'S MY OWN FAULT.
I CHOSE TO BE HERE.
AND AS MUCH AS I WANT TO SCREAM... THEY CAN'T HEAR ME.
I'M TOO SMALL.

CHAPTER 26

IT'S ALWAYS BEEN LIKE THIS, AFTER ALL...
ARE YOU READY, NICO?
YES.
WELL, THEN...
HERE IT COMES!
OH.
POW
NICO...?
WAAAH!
SO YOU'RE GOING TO TAKE CARE OF THE CHILD?
I HAVE NO CHOICE, EVANS.
HIS MOTHER DIED PROTECTING ME.
DAD, NICO GOT HURT!!
WE'RE HAVING A CONVERSATION, MARK—
BUT HE'S BLEEDING!
WAAHH!
THERE'S A FIRST AID KIT UNDER THE COUNTER.

I COULD TAKE CARE OF HIM, PENDRAGON.
MARK WOULD BE HAPPY TO HAVE A LITTLE BROTHER.
YOU CAN'T POSSIBLY TAKE CARE OF TWO CHILDREN BY YOURSELF.
WHEN HIS MOTHER CAME ASKING FOR HELP, THE CHILD WAS DYING.
I SAVED HIM WITH MY MAGIC, AND HIS MOTHER WAS ACCUSED OF WITCHCRAFT.
SHE DIDN'T BETRAY ME, SO THEY BURNED HER.
I CAN'T LEAVE THE CHILD. HE'S AN ORPHAN BECAUSE OF ME.
BUT I CAN'T LET HIM GET TOO ATTACHED—I DON'T WANT TO ENDANGER HIM, TOO.
EVERYONE WHO COMES NEAR ME GETS HURT.
NICO! LOOK!
YOU'RE HEALED NOW.
IT STILL H-HURTS.
HUH?
PAIN FADES, NICO.
AND THIS BAND-AID IS EVIDENCE.
EVIDENCE?
YES! A WOUND IS EVIDENCE OF COURAGE.

GETTING HURT ISN'T FUN.
BUT SCARS ARE COOL. PIRATES HAVE TONS OF THEM.
YOU'RE A TOUGH GUY, NICO!
OH.
I THINK I'VE ALWAYS BEEN LIKE THIS.
...WANTING TO BE GOOD ENOUGH.
LOOK WHAT I DREW!
DAD
I WANTED THE MASTER TO BE PROUD OF ME.
...
IT'S NICE. BUT CALL ME PENDRAGON, NICO.
I'M NOT YOUR FATHER.
BUT AS MUCH AS I TRIED, IT WAS NEVER ENOUGH.
IS THAT A DRAGON, DAD?
DON'T CALL ME DAD!

I'M SORRY.
AND I'VE TOLD YOU NOT TO BOTHER ME WHEN I'M DOING MAGIC!
MAGIC IS DANGEROUS!
WE WOULD NEVER BE A FAMILY.
I WASN'T HIS SON. HE WASN'T MY FATHER.
WELL, I'M DETERMINED TO LEARN HOW TO DO MAGIC!
AND I'LL BE A GREAT WITCH AND HELP YOU WITH YOUR DIVINATION!
SO I CHOSE...
...TO BECOME HIS PUPIL.
MASTER PENDRAGON REFUSED TO TEACH ME, SO I TAUGHT MYSELF.
BOOM
DESPITE THAT...
ALL MY ATTEMPTS TO DO MAGIC WERE AN UTTER DISASTER.
I SPENT HOURS, ENTIRE DAYS...
WEEKS. MONTHS.
YEARS.
STUDYING BY MYSELF.
PRACTICING.
TRYING THINGS OVER AND OVER.
BUT I ALWAYS ENDED UP WITH THE SAME RESULT.

NOTHING.
NOTHING.
NOTHING.
NOTHING.
NOTHING.
I JUST WANTED HIM
TO BE PROUD OF ME.
BUT IT WAS USELESS.
I WAS MISERABLE.

WHAT HAPPENED TO YOU YESTERDAY?
WE WERE SUPPOSED TO MEET UP!
I'M SORRY.
I WAS JUST STUDYING...
I THINK I'LL HAVE TO REPEAT THIS YEAR.
I'VE BEEN SO FOCUSED ON MAGIC...
LOOK, MARK EVANS!
HE'S SO CUTE.
I'LL HAVE TO HANG OUT WITH YOUNGER KIDS. SO BORING.
AND HE'S SO TALL AND STRONG...
AND COOL!
I DON'T UNDERSTAND WHY HE HANGS OUT WITH THAT CARROT TOP, NICO.
THEY'RE SO DIFFERENT!
NICO IS TOO CONCEITED.
YEAH...
I THINK NICO STICKS TO EVANS BECAUSE HE WANTS TO BE POPULAR.
AND EVANS IS TOO NICE TO SAY NO.
I WAS NEVER GOOD ENOUGH.
I ALWAYS ENDED UP MAKING A FOOL OF MYSELF.
I FELT INCREDIBLY LONELY.
AND ALL OF A SUDDEN,
MARK WAS THE TALL ONE, THE CUTE ONE, THE POPULAR ONE, AND EVEN THE SMART ONE.

IT CAN'T BE...
MASTER...
WHY ARE YOU UP SO EARLY?
OBSERVE, NICO.
HUH?
HE CAST THE SPELL PERFECTLY, AFTER READING IT JUST ONCE?
TRULY INCREDIBLE. THESE CHILDREN HAVE ENORMOUS POWER.
I WILL ADOPT THEM AS MY PUPILS.
WHAT ARE YOU TALKING ABOUT, MASTER?
YOU SAID YOU DIDN'T NEED A PUPIL.
THIS IS DIFFERENT.
WHAT?

SOMEONE NEEDS TO GUIDE ALL OF THEIR POTENTIAL.
BUT MASTER...
...I'M YOUR PUPIL.
AND YOU CAN'T DO MAGIC.
I FELT SICK.
DON'T WORRY, YOU CAN STILL LIVE HERE IF YOU WANT.
HE HAD REPLACED ME.
OH.
HEY
I RAN AWAY FROM THE MASTER'S HOUSE.
THAT'S WHEN I REALLY STARTED TO SCREW THINGS UP.

AREN'T YOU GONNA TELL ME WHAT HAPPENED?
NAH, NEVER MIND. THE MASTER IS AN IDIOT.
MAN, YOU'RE CRANKY.
AND DON'T TELL MASTER PENDRAGON I'M HERE!
HOW LONG WILL YOU BE STAYING?
I DON'T KNOW. BUT I'LL NEVER GO BACK TO LIVE WITH THE MASTER AGAIN!
YOU SHOULD HELP ME, YOU'RE SUPPOSED TO BE MY FRIEND.
OKAY, OKAY... SO MUCH TEEN ANGST.
LONG TIME NO SEE, PENDRAGON! YOU DON'T LOOK VERY GOOD.
I'VE BEEN TOLD THAT NICO IS LIVING HERE.
MASTER...
I WON'T COME HOME, MASTER, NO MATTER HOW MUCH YOU INSIST!
WELL, TRUTHFULLY...

I THINK IT WOULD BE BETTER FOR YOU NOT TO COME BACK.
MAYBE IT'S BEST YOU STAY WITH THE EVANSES.
WHAT ARE YOU TALKING ABOUT, PENDRAGON?
DON'T WORRY, EVANS. I'LL GIVE YOU MONEY TO HELP OUT WITH EXPENSES.
BUT—
I DIDN'T MEAN *THAT!*
FORGET YOU, MASTER!
NICO...
NICO!
I HATE HIM.
I HATE HIM.
I HATE HIM.
NICO—
I HATE YOU!
I TOLD YOU NOT TO SAY ANYTHING. NOW LOOK WHAT HAPPENED! IT'S YOUR FAULT!
WHAT?
I KNEW I WAS SCREWING THINGS UP.
DO YOU THINK YOU CAN MAKE DECISIONS FOR ME?
I KNEW IT WASN'T MARK'S FAULT.

STOP BEHAVING LIKE AN IDIOT, OKAY?
I WAS ONLY TRYING TO HELP YOU!
!
LET ME GO.
I KNEW IT, AND EVEN SO...
I DON'T NEED YOUR HELP ANYMORE, OKAY? I DON'T NEED YOU ANYMORE.
I TOOK IT OUT ON HIM.
AND, SHORTLY AFTER...
I MET THEM.
YOU ALMOST HIT MY FACE!
I COULD HAVE TRICKED THE MASTER.
BUT I DECIDED TO PRETEND I DIDN'T CARE.

I PREFERRED TO TRICK MYSELF.
HATING THEM WAS EASY.
WELL, IT WASN'T THAT EASY WITH DANI.
SHE'S CLUMSY
AND CUTE.
BUT DORIAN...
DORIAN WAS MY NIGHTMARE.
HE HAD EVERYTHING I WANTED.
HE MADE IT LOOK SO EASY.
HE WAS CONSTANTLY SHOWING OFF. IT WAS UNBEARABLE.
AND THE WORST THING WAS...
HE LOOKED UP TO ME. HE ADMIRED ME.
ARE YOU GONNA HANG OUT WITH YOUR FRIENDS?
CAN I JOIN?
I COULDN'T LET HIM TAKE ANYTHING MORE FROM ME.

ANNOYING.
I WILL ASK THE MASTER TO LEND ME A PAIR OF BOOTS.
IT PISSED ME OFF.
DON'T TOUCH ME! I TOLD YOU I DON'T LIKE YOU!
LEAVE MY BROTHER ALONE!
AT THAT POINT, MY PUNISHMENT ARRIVED.
THERE'S NO DOUBT... DORIAN OR DANI...
THE KING OF THE WITCHES IS ONE OF THEM.
IT WAS LIKE A BAD JOKE.
I LEARNED WHAT USELESS TRULY MEANS.
AND THE WORST PART OF IT WAS...
...PERHAPS THE MASTER HAD ONLY TRIED TO KEEP ME SAFE. PERHAPS I MEANT SOMETHING TO HIM.
BUT IT WAS TOO LATE. I LET HIM DOWN, I MESSED THINGS UP WITH DORIAN. I PUSHED EVERYONE AWAY.
BECAUSE I WAS TOO PROUD.
AND NOW...

HEY.
HEY.
WHAT HAPPENED?
I SHOUTED AT DANI AND RAN OFF.
I SEE.
MARK...
DO YOU HATE ME?
THAT'S MY LINE.
I THOUGHT YOU DIDN'T NEED ME ANYMORE.
I WAS JUST ANGRY. AT EVERYTHING.
COMPARED TO YOU, I FELT LIKE AN IDIOT.
NICO, YOU'RE THE ONLY ONE WHO THINKS I'M COOL.
THAT'S THE WORST PART,
YOU DON'T EVEN REALIZE HOW MUCH PEOPLE LIKE YOU.
I SAID THOSE HORRIBLE THINGS BECAUSE I WAS HURT.
WELL, YOU'VE BEEN SAYING THEM FOR MONTHS NOW...
I COULDN'T APOLOGIZE AS IF NOTHING HAD HAPPENED! I HAVE MY PRIDE.
DUDE... SERIOUSLY?
I DON'T HATE YOU, MARK.
YOU'RE MY BEST FRIEND.
I'M SORRY.

!
STOP GRINNING LIKE THAT!
I WASN'T GRINNING!
I THINK YOU'RE REALLY COOL, NICO.
AND I'M NOT THE ONLY ONE.
OH REALLY?
WHO ELSE CAN EVEN STAND ME?
YOU KNOW PERFECTLY WELL WHO I'M TALKING ABOUT.
IT WAS REALLY FUN!
...
NICO...
WE ALMOST HAD THAT GOLDEN GOOSE TRAPPED.
LAST TIME I TRIED TO STEAL AN EGG, IT WAS A DISASTER.
WRAPPING OUR SHOES IN PLASTIC BAGS WAS A GREAT IDEA, DORIAN.
MY FEET ARE NEAT!
BUT THE REST OF YOU IS COVERED IN MUD...
DORIAN! FINALLY.
HOW COULD YOU SPEND THE NIGHT OUT WITHOUT WARNING ME?
AGH!
WHAT ABOUT OUR POTION?

I'M SORRY, BUT WE CLIMBED UP A BEANSTALK AND THERE WAS A GIANT—
SURE, A GIANT.
LOOK, DANI!
UGH.
NICO!
YOU BOTH HAD ME WORRIED SICK.
I'M SORRY, NICO, I'LL TRY TO FIX THE CURSE.
I JUST NEED MORE TIME.
COME ON, NICO.
FINE.
I'D LIKE TO SPEAK TO DORIAN, PLEASE. ALONE.
PAY ATTENTION, BECAUSE I'M NOT SAYING THIS TWICE.
AHEM—
JUST A SECOND! I HAVE SOMETHING FOR YOU.
LOOK!
WHAT ARE THOSE?
MAGIC BEANS.
A GUY PLANTED THEM AND A GIANT BEANSTALK GREW.
WE COULD USE THEM TO CREATE A POTION FOR YOU, DON'T YOU THINK?
DORIAN...
WHY ARE YOU SO NICE TO ME?

CHAPTER 27

DON'T EAVESDROP, MONICA! NICO ASKED FOR PRIVACY.
YOU'RE FREE TO GO, IF YOU'RE NOT CURIOUS.
MAKE SOME ROOM.
HEY, NOW I CAN'T SEE ANYTHING!
SHHH. DON'T TALK SO LOUD, THEY'LL HEAR US.
I'M SORRY.
WHAT?
I SAID I'M SORRY—
HUH?
NICO, IF YOU DON'T SPEAK LOUDER I WON'T UNDERSTAND YOU!
I SAID I'M SORRY, ALL RIGHT?! I'M SORRY I WAS SUCH A JERK TO YOU!
I'M JEALOUS! I'M MEAN TO YOU BECAUSE I'M ENVIOUS, OKAY?!
WHAT?
YOU HAVE NOTHING TO ENVY, NICO.

IT SHOULD BE THE OTHER WAY AROUND.
UUUUGH.
SNIFF.
P-PLEASE DON'T CRY...
WHY WOULD YOU SAY THAT?
YOU'RE ALWAYS SHOWING OFF HOW GOOD YOU ARE AT MAGIC.
MAGIC?
HE'S CRYING! SHOULD WE DO SOMETHING?
NO, LET THEM BE.
OH, HOW LOVELY!
IF YOU WANT TO LEARN SOME MAGIC, I CAN TEACH YOU. I'M GIVING LESSONS TO MONICA AS WELL.
IT'S NOT THAT.
I ALREADY KNOW I CAN'T DO MAGIC...
BUT I SHOULDN'T HAVE TAKEN IT OUT ON YOU.
I WANT US TO BE FRIENDS!
...
IF YOU FORGIVE ME...
WE CAN START FRESH.

WHOA!
THE SPELL BROKE?
BUT HOW?
I DON'T KNOW... I...
JUST SAID I WAS SORRY... AND ALL OF A SUDDEN—
YOU MUST HAVE BEEN CURSED!
CURSES CAN BE BROKEN WITH CERTAIN ACTIONS.
DORIAN EXPLAINED THAT TO ME YESTERDAY.
THAT'S TRUE!
IT LOOKS LIKE DANI IS AN EXPERT IN CURSES.
HUH?
YOU'RE GOING TOO FAR.
WHAT?
IT'S OKAY... SHE'S RIGHT.
I DIDN'T MEAN IT BADLY!
...

LET ME THROUGH—
WHAT ARE YOU DOING?
AAAAGH!
COME ON, DANI!
WHA—
LET'S HAVE A BROOM RACE.
WE NEED TO CELEBRATE!
BUT NICO...
I'M NOT A WITCH ANYMORE, YOU KNOW THAT.
I REMOVED YOUR CURSE MYSELF, SO YOU OWE ME ONE.
DORIAN, HELP ME OR I'LL CRASH.
HERE WE GO!
HURRY UP, I'M ALREADY WINNING!

THANKS, DUDE.
I'M HAVING DÉJÀ VU.
JUST A DROP OF THIS AND IT'LL BE READY...
potion:
ners level
Useful to treat mild sickness
It is also an antidote to
many types of venom.
Ingredients:
ALL RIGHT, MONICA...
LET'S MAKE OUR POTION!
BOOM
IS THIS NORMAL?
YES, ABSOLUTELY.
YOU TRICKED ME!
HA HA HA, NO WAY!
WHO'S GONNA TRY THE POTION?
YOU DIDN'T THINK ABOUT THAT, RIGHT?
OF COURSE...
IF NOBODY TRIES IT, WE WON'T KNOW IF IT WORKS.
SINCE IT WAS YOUR IDEA, MARK—
NO.

WHY NOT?
LAST TIME I TRIED A POTION, I SPENT A WEEK TRYING TO KILL DANI.
GOOD POINT.
MONICA, WHAT ARE YOU DOING?
MAKE YOURSELF USEFUL. WE CAN PRACTICE YOUR DANCING.
TOMORROW WE'RE ATTENDING THE GREAT BALL AT THE PALACE, REMEMBER.
TOMORROW?!
DID YOU SERIOUSLY FORGET ABOUT IT?
MAYBE IT WOULD BE GOOD TO PRACTICE A BIT.
JUST DO YOUR BEST, MARK.
HOW CAN THEY BE SO CALM?
I CAN'T STOP THINKING ABOUT THE PARTY AND WHO I MIGHT SEE THERE...

DANI WON THE RACE, THEN?
OF COURSE!
LAUGH IT UP, MARK, BUT AT LEAST I'M NOT *DANCING* WITH MY BROOM.
SINCE YOU'RE BACK TO NORMAL, YOU CAN PRACTICE DANCING LIKE EVERYONE ELSE.
YOU DON'T WANT TO MAKE A FOOL OF YOURSELF AT THE PARTY...
DORIAN...
WHAT ARE YOU DOING?
IT'D BE SUCH A SHAME IF NO ONE TRIED YOUR POTION...
SO I THOUGHT WE COULD BOTH TRY IT, FIFTY-FIFTY.
I'M SURE IT'LL WORK PERFECTLY.
AFTER ALL, I'M YOUR TEACHER.
WE'RE IN THIS TOGETHER.
WHY...
...IS HE SO CUTE?!
SINCE IT'S AN ANTIDOTE, WE'LL NEED SOME VENOM FIRST. SOMETHING HARMLESS, THOUGH...
HANG ON.
YOU WANT US TO POISON OURSELVES??
I'VE READ ENOUGH NOVELS TO KNOW HOW THIS ENDS!
HUH?
WE DON'T REALLY NEED TO DRINK IT NOW, IF WE'RE SURE WE DID IT RIGHT.
GIVE ME YOUR VIAL!

VOILÀ!
A NECKLACE?
CORRECT! WE'LL ALWAYS HAVE THE ANTIDOTE WITH US IN CASE WE NEED IT.
YOU'RE GIVING IT TO ME?
OF COURSE... WE'RE A TEAM, RIGHT?
IT'S LIKE CARRYING AN AMULET.
IT'S COOL.
THANK YOU.
IS HE DOING THIS ON PURPOSE?
WHAT ON EARTH ARE YOU THINKING, MONICA?
MY HEAD HURTS!
WE NEED TO LEARN THIS BY TOMORROW EVENING!
WOULDN'T IT BE MORE LOGICAL TO PRACTICE TOGETHER?
WHO SHOULD I DANCE WITH, THEN?
DON'T LOOK AT ME. I SAW YOU STOMPING ON THE PRINCESS'S FEET...
I'LL PASS...
DORIAN! WILL YOU PRACTICE WITH ME?
OH, YOU'VE REMEMBERED YOU HAVE A BROTHER.
HUH?
YOU WON'T EVEN TOUCH A WAND FOR ME, BUT YOU'LL HAVE BROOM RACES WITH ANYONE WHO ASKS.

YOU'RE STILL MAD?
YES.
TELL ME, DORIAN...
HOW OLD ARE YOU?
!
ALMOST 13...
WHY?
OH! SO YOU'RE ONLY 12?
YOU'RE JUST A LITTLE KID, AFTER ALL.
EH?!
A LITTLE KID?
AND WHAT ARE YOU SUPPOSED TO BE?
I'M 14. I'M A TEENAGER.
HE HE
OF COURSE DORIAN IS CUTE.
LIKE A PUPPY'S CUTE.
YES, BUT...
I'LL BE 13 SOON, YOU KNOW?
WHAT IS THAT SUPPOSED TO MEAN?!
WHAT DO YOU MEAN?
I'M SICK OF YOU!
BUT YOU STARTED—
PUFF
I'M GOING TO SLEEP!

CHAPTER 28

I'M SO HAPPY TO BE GOING WITH YOU ALL.
I'VE BEEN PRACTICING MY DANCE SKILLS ALL DAY.
MM-HMM...
ARE YOU OKAY, PRINCESS? YOU LOOK UPSET.
I'M KINDA NERVOUS...
I WONDER IF WILLIAM WILL BE THERE.
I'M SURE OF IT! DON'T WORRY.
I'M READY. PLEASE, DON'T LAUGH.
OOH, LOOK AT YOU!
I'M THE BEST AT PICKING OUTFITS!
HA HA HA
YOU'RE JUST JEALOUS.
I TOLD YOU NOT TO LAUGH!
MATCHING YOUR DATE IS IDEAL FOR THESE KINDS OF PARTIES.
WHY IS NICO WEARING GREEN, THEN?
BECAUSE CARLO'S MY DATE, OF COURSE.

WAIT FOR US!
ISN'T MY HAT EXTREMELY COOL?
IT LOOKS LIKE YOU COULD PULL A RABBIT OUT OF IT AT ANY MOMENT.
...
AHEM... MONICA...
YOU LOOK VERY ELEGANT TODAY.
!!
WE SHOULD GET GOING.
?
?
WEAPONS ARE FORBIDDEN INSIDE THE TOWN.
THAT'S NOT A WEAPON, IT'S MY WAND!
THOSE ARE THE RULES, BOY.
THAT LITTLE DEMON CAN'T ENTER EITHER.
HUH?
I THINK HE MEANS CARLO.
EXCUSE ME, DO YOU KNOW WHO YOU'RE TALKING TO?
I'M PRINCESS MONICA!

GOOD NEWS! YOU'RE ALL V.I.P.S NOW.
FOLLOW ME!
THEY'RE HERE...
MY DAUGHTER...
AND THE OTHER CHILDREN, TOO.
ARE YOU SURE THIS IS THE RIGHT THING TO DO?
YES, YOUR MAJESTY.
THE WYTTE FAMILY IS DANGEROUS.
WELCOME TO MY HUMBLE ABODE.

IT'S FULL OF FANCY RICH PEOPLE. LET'S GET OUT OF HERE.
DON'T WORRY, MARK, YOU FIT RIGHT IN.
WILL WE MEET KING GEORGE IN PERSON?
DO YOU THINK HE'LL PAY ME FOR MY BODYGUARD SERVICES?
OF COURSE. WAIT HERE, I'LL GO LOOK FOR HIM.
THAT WON'T BE NECESSARY.
DADDY!
I MISSED YOU!
I MISSED YOU TOO.
DO I REALLY NEED TO LOSE TRACK OF YOU FOR WEEKS TO GET A HUG?
I HAVE SO MUCH TO TELL YOU!
I SEE THAT.
BUT FIRST...
YOU TWO.

DORIAN AND DANIELA WYTTE, RIGHT?
YES, YOUR MAJESTY.
DADDY...?
GUARDS!
ISN'T THAT THE KING?
WHAT HAPPENED?
A FIGHT?
THIS WHOLE THING WAS A SETUP, WASN'T IT?
WHATEVER YOU'VE HEARD ABOUT THE WYTTES...
YOU DON'T KNOW THEM.
THEY WOULD NEVER HURT ANYBODY.
THEY'RE MY FRIENDS.
DON'T HURT THEM.
I WON'T LET YOU KILL THEM!

I DON'T WANT TO KILL YOUR FRIENDS.
HUH?
PENDRAGON TOLD ME EVERYTHING.
I AM AWARE OF THE REBELLION LED BY THE WYTTES,
AND THAT ONE OF THEIR CHILDREN IS DESTINED TO DETHRONE ME.
MASTER!
BUT PENDRAGON ALSO TOLD ME THAT YOU ARE KIND, INCAPABLE OF HURTING OTHERS.
SO I'M PLANNING TO KEEP YOU FAR AWAY FROM YOUR PARENTS' INFLUENCE.
YOU'RE GOING TO LIVE HERE, AT THE PALACE.
I DON'T WANT ANOTHER WAR.
AND I WOULD NEVER KILL A CHILD.
I WILL PROTECT YOU. ALL OF YOU.
THE BALL ISN'T A SETUP...
IT'S SUPPOSED TO SEND A MESSAGE OF PEACE.
TO SHOW THE WORLD THAT WITCHES AND NON-MAGICAL PEOPLE CAN LIVE IN HARMONY.
WE'VE BEEN FIGHTING FOR YEARS, AND HAVE LOST SO MANY PEOPLE.
WE'VE FORGOTTEN THAT WE ARE ALL HUMAN BEINGS.

THAT'S WHY I'M OPENING THE DOORS OF MY HOME TODAY. TO EVERYONE.
LET'S EAT, DANCE, AND LAUGH TOGETHER.
LEAVING WAR BEHIND ONCE AND FOR ALL.
YOU'RE GOING TO LIVE HERE WITH ME! HOW EXCITING!
IT WILL BE SO MUCH FUN.
WHAT ABOUT ME, MASTER?
I'VE BEEN ENTRUSTED WITH FINDING THE MISSING PRINCES.
MEANWHILE, YOU CAN STAY HERE.
Y-YOU SHOULD STAY TOO, MARK!
ARE YOU EXCITED, DORIAN?
!
WHY ARE YOU STARING AT ME LIKE THAT?
I WAS SURE YOU WOULD USE THE PARTY AS AN EXCUSE TO GO BACK TO THE PALACE AND LEAVE THE MASTER'S HOUSE.
I WAS SO SCARED... BUT NOW YOU'RE SMILING AS YOU ALWAYS DO.
UH...

I'M SO RELIEVED.
D-DORIAN.
WE MUST GO TO THE PARTY. THE OTHERS HAVE LEFT ALREADY!
OKAY...
?
NOT SO FAST, MY PRINCE!
IT CAN'T BE...
HIM?
LONG TIME NO SEE!
IT'S THE GUY WHO WAS WITH WILLIAM...
HE'LL RECOGNIZE ME!
OH... IT'S JUST YOU, AMIR.
I'M HAPPY TO SEE YOU, TOO.
TELL ME...
IS WILLIAM HERE SOMEWHERE?
NO... WELL, I DON'T KNOW.
IS THAT SO?
HE WOULDN'T MISS A GOOD PARTY. IF HE HAD ESCAPED, HE WOULD BE HERE FOR SURE.
AND WHAT ABOUT DAMIEN?

I DON'T KNOW ANYTHING. I'VE BEEN AWAY FOR A WHILE AND JUST GOT BACK TO THE PALACE.
SORRY, I DIDN'T KNOW.
I WAS KIDNAPPED ALONG WITH WILLIAM AND THE OTHER PRINCES. HE AND I MANAGED TO ESCAPE.
BUT WILLIAM DIDN'T WANT TO ABANDON THE OTHERS, SO HE GOT ON A GREEN DRAGON AND WENT BACK FOR THEM.
DOES MAGIC.
WELL-DRESSED.
RIDES DRAGONS.
A PRINCE.
FIGHTS WITH SWORDS
IS BRAVE
AND HANDSOME AND CHARMING.
AND TALL.
HE GOT ON A DRAGON?!
WELL, ACTUALLY, IT'S MORE ACCURATE TO SAY THAT THE DRAGON TOOK HIM.
DOES MAGIC.
WELL-DRESSED.
RIDES DRAGONS.
RIDES DRAGONS.
A PRINCE.
FIGHTS WITH SWORDS
IS BRAVE
AND HANDSOME AND CHARMING.
AND TALL
BUT I'M HAPPY TO SEE YOU'RE DOING JUST FINE, MONICA.
I COULD ALWAYS MARRY YOU IF WILLIAM DOESN'T COME BACK.
WILLIAM *WILL* COME BACK.
I'M SURE OF IT.
AND IF HE DOESN'T, I'LL KEEP LOOKING UNTIL I FIND HIM.
WHEN I DO, I'LL MARRY HIM. NOT YOU, NOT ANYBODY ELSE.
NOW IF YOU'LL EXCUSE ME.

NOW THIS IS LUXURY.
THIS MUFFIN SUCKS.
WHERE ARE MONICA AND DORIAN?
WOULD YOU LIKE TO DANCE WITH ONE OF US?
ER... NO, THANKS.
HOW CUTE, HE'S BLUSHING.
COME ON, DANCE WITH US!
NO. SHE IS.
I'M SORRY, GIRLS, BUT HE ALREADY PROMISED THE FIRST DANCE TO SOMEONE ELSE.
IS THAT SO? ARE YOU HIS PARTNER, LITTLE GIRL?
MONICA!
FINALLY!
ANNE! IVY!
YOU SAID YOU WERE LOOKING FOR YOUR PRINCE AND YOU CAME BACK WITH A NEW ONE!
IT'S NOT LIKE THAT.
NOW THAT WE'RE ALL HERE, LET'S DANCE!
COME ON, MARK.
YOU HAVE TO TASTE THIS CHOCOLATE CAKE, DORIAN!

NO WAY.
COME ON, MARK, DON'T BE A PARTY POOPER.
WHAT ABOUT YOU, DORIAN?
WILL YOU DANCE WITH ME ?
WHAT?
WELL...
WE'RE NOT MATCHING. AND I NEED TO DANCE WITH DANI, SO—
DON'T WORRY, PRINCESS. I'LL DANCE WITH YOU!
THANK YOU SO MUCH, NICO!
I DIDN'T PRACTICE JUST TO SIT ALL NIGHT!

CHAPTER 29

YOU LOOK BORED, MARK.
!
DO YOU WANT TO GO DOWNTOWN? THERE'S A PARTY IN THE VILLAGE.
YES, I NEED A PROPER PARTY!
DORIAN, SHALL WE DANCE BEFORE WE LEAVE?
I DON'T FEEL LIKE IT.
BESIDES... DON'T YOU LIKE MARK?
WHY DID YOU CHOOSE ME AS YOUR DANCE PARTNER?
MARK IS CUTE AND EVERYTHING...
BUT YOU'RE MY FAVORITE PERSON! YOU KNOW THAT.
I WANTED TO HAVE SOME FUN WITH YOU.
I ALSO MISSED WEARING MATCHING OUTFITS.
SHUT UP.
HA! ARE YOU EMBARRASSED NOW?
SINCE DORIAN IS BEING SUCH A DOWNER, I'LL DANCE WITH YOU!
WE'D BETTER GO LOOK FOR MONICA INSTEAD...
BE RIGHT BACK!
BUT...

BY THE WAY, WHAT'S WRONG WITH YOU?
WHY DON'T YOU WANT TO DANCE?
WELL, ACTUALLY...
I KNOW IT'S HARD TO BELIEVE, BUT I LIED.
I CAN'T DANCE!
I'VE READ A BUNCH OF BOOKS BUT I DIDN'T PRACTICE.
IT'S NOT HARD TO BELIEVE AT ALL.
YOU CAN'T SWIM EITHER.
OR FLY ON A BROOM.
YOU'RE CLUMSY, SLOW—
I'M AN UTTER DISASTER.
HAHA, YES YOU A—
"I WANNA BE FRIENDS!"
AH.
DON'T DESPAIR.
WE ALL HAVE THINGS WE'RE GOOD OR BAD AT.
IF YOU WORK HARD AT IT, I'M SURE YOU'LL GET WHAT YOU WANT!
YOU'RE RIGHT, NICO. I JUST NEED TO BELIEVE IN MYSELF!
I'M SO HAPPY WE'RE FRIENDS.
HE BOUGHT IT?!
AHEM... EXCUSE ME.
WOULD YOU BE SO KIND AS TO DANCE WITH ME?

YOU SHOULD HAVE SEEN HER DRESS!
I CAN'T BELIEVE I MISSED IT.
MONICA! WE'RE ALL GOING TO THE VILLAGE. ARE YOU COMING?
I'D BETTER STAY HERE.
IS THIS REALLY YOUR FIRST TIME DANCING?
YOU'RE DOING REALLY WELL!
THANK YOU. I'VE READ A LOT OF BOOKS ABOUT IT.
HEY, LOOK AT YOUR FRIEND! I THOUGHT HE WAS A WEIRDO, BUT HE CAN REALLY DANCE.
DIDN'T HE SAY THAT HE WASN'T IN THE MOOD TO DANCE?
MAYBE HE DIDN'T WANT TO DANCE WITH ME...
LET'S HEAD TO THE VILLAGE.
WHAT ABOUT THE PRINCESS? AND DORIAN?
MONICA WANTS TO STAY.
DORIAN IS STILL ANGRY AT ME.
WE'LL HAVE FUN, JUST THE THREE OF US.
LET THE PARTY BEGIN!

NOW, THIS IS WHAT I'M TALKING ABOUT.
PEOPLE ARE HAVING SO MUCH FUN.
AND THERE ARE TONS OF WITCHES!
OH.
HEY!
THE LITTLE WITCH!
ALEX!
COME ON, JUMP IN!
OH, LITTLE GOBLIN, YOU'RE HERE TOO!
SING WITH ME!
I DON'T KNOW THIS SONG.
COME ON, NICO, SING FOR US!

THAT WAS SO COOL, GUYS.
ALL THANKS TO MY IMPROVISATION.
MARK, YOU MISSED THE CONCERT!
YEAH, I SAW YOU. AND HEARD NICO'S AWFUL SINGING.
THEY'RE PLAYING DARTS AND CARDS OVER THERE, LET'S GO!
IT'S SO FUN TO BE ALL HERE TOGETHER...
I WISH DORIAN AND MONICA WERE HERE TOO.
BUT...
...I'M SURE HE'S HAVING FUN WITHOUT ME.
WHERE DID EVERYBODY GO?
IF YOU'RE LOOKING FOR YOUR FRIENDS...
THEY ALL WENT TO THE VILLAGE.
WHAT? DANI WOULDN'T LEAVE ME BEHIND.
HEY, IVY! OH, MONICA, YOU LOOK ANGRY...
COME WITH ME! I NEED TO TALK TO YOU FOR A SECOND.
WHAT'S WRONG?
IT'S OKAY.
IT'S NORMAL TO BE ANGRY. IT DOESN'T HAVE TO MEAN ANYTHING.
DORIAN, YOU...
YOU CAN DANCE!

OF COURSE I CAN! I SAID SO A THOUSAND TIMES.
THEN WHY DIDN'T YOU WANT TO DANCE WITH ME?!
YOU'RE REALLY TALL FOR A 12 YEAR OLD.
I ALREADY TOLD YOU... WE DON'T MATCH.
WHAT A LAME EXCUSE! YOU DANCED WITH ANNE AND YOUR OUTFITS DON'T MATCH, EITHER.
I WASN'T REFERRING TO THAT.
I'M... TOO SHORT.
WHAT? THAT'S NOT TRUE!
WELL, EVEN SO...
I'M STILL SHORTER THAN YOU.
ONLY A FEW INCHES, BUT I DON'T WANT TO LOOK LIKE A SHRIMP—
MY FATHER ALWAYS SAYS THAT—
!
MONICA?
STEP

WHO...?
OH.
DAMIEN.
DID FATHER SEND YOU?
TELL ME!
!
WHY ARE YOU HERE, DORIAN?!
WAIT, DAMIEN—
BE CAREFUL, PRINCESS, THIS BOY IS DANGEROUS.
NO, HE ISN'T!

YOU'RE THE ONLY DANGEROUS ONE HERE.
WHAT?
I KNOW YOU'RE GAINING THE KING'S TRUST. YOU'RE PLANNING TO USURP THE THRONE.
AND I WON'T ALLOW IT.
DO YOU SERIOUSLY THINK YOU CAN BLAME ME FOR EVERYTHING AND NO ONE WILL SUSPECT YOU?
THINK AGAIN, KING OF WITCHES!
UGH.
I FOUND YOUR BACKPACK ON THE FLOATING ROCK. I SAW THE CURSES YOU WERE KEEPING INSIDE.
...WHAT?
MY BLOOD RAN COLD.

TORTURE, DEATH... IS THAT WHAT YOU USE YOUR MAGIC FOR?
WHO ARE YOU GOING TO HURT, DORIAN?
BUT YOU'RE THE GOOD ONE OF US?
YOU'RE JUST LIKE DAD. A MANIPULATOR.
THAT'S WHY I LEFT.
I'M NOT THE ONE POINTING A WAND AT HIS LITTLE BROTHER.
DAD TOLD ME YOU WERE A COWARD WHO RAN AWAY.
AND I TRUST HIM BEFORE YOU.
DAMIEN!
YOU'RE BROTHERS. THIS ISN'T RIGHT!
HE'S DANGEROUS!
HE WANTS TO KILL YOUR FATHER!
NO.
I LIED.

I SAID DAMIEN COULD BE THE KING OF WITCHES TO PROTECT DORIAN AND DANI.
BUT I CAN'T FIND A SINGLE REASON NOT TO TRUST HIM.
I THINK BOTH THE MASTER AND THE PROPHECY ARE WRONG.
IT WOULDN'T MAKE SENSE FOR ANY OF YOU THREE TO SUDDENLY TURN EVIL.
THAT'S WHY I DON'T WANT YOU TO FIGHT...
HUH?
EXCUSE ME FOR WHAT I'M ABOUT TO SAY, PRINCESS...
BUT YOU'RE NOTHING MORE THAN A SPOILED BRAT.
YOU BEHAVE LIKE AN IMMATURE CHILD, AND YOU DON'T TAKE ANY OF THIS SERIOUSLY.
OF COURSE I DO! I'M REALLY WORRIED.
I SAW YOU EARLIER, DANCING AND GIGGLING WITH THAT GINGER BOYFRIEND OF YOURS.
I DESERVE TO HAVE A GOOD TIME ONCE IN A WHILE!
NO, YOU DON'T!
NOT WHILE WILL COULD...

...NOT WHILE WILL COULD BE DEAD.
WILL'S FINE.
YOU'RE TOO NAÏVE.
AND DORIAN...
I'M NOT SURE IF YOU'RE INNOCENT OR NOT. BUT IF YOU KNEW WHAT OUR FATHER WAS CAPABLE OF...
BUT WE'LL KNOW THE TRUTH SOON.
IT'S ALMOST MIDNIGHT.
WHY DOES THAT MATTER?
DON'T YOU KNOW?
MIDNIGHT...
IS THE WITCHING HOUR.

DORIAN—
I'M FINE.
JUST... A LITTLE CONFUSED.
OKAY.
AND YOU?
I'D BETTER GO TO SLEEP.
NOW?
DAMIEN'S RIGHT.
I SHOULDN'T ACT AS IF NOTHING HAPPENED.
I'M GOING TO BED, AND FIRST THING TOMORROW I'LL GO LOOK FOR WILLIAM.
I WON'T GET DISTRACTED THIS TIME, EITHER.
MONICA, WAIT!
I REALLY WOULD LIKE TO DANCE WITH YOU.
NOW?
WHATEVER HAPPENS, GOOD OR BAD, WE PROBABLY WON'T HAVE ANOTHER CHANCE TO DANCE TOGETHER.
THIS COULD BE THE ONLY TIME.
SO...
YES. I DO WANT TO.
RIGHT.
WOW, MARK WON AGAIN!
THAT'S IMPRESSIVE!
HE'S REALLY STRONG.
GO MARK!
!

I'M UP NEXT!
BLAM
YOU, NICO?
WHAT ABOUT IT?
LOOKS LIKE SOMEONE'S FEELING COMPETITIVE.
NICO IS ALWAYS LIKE THAT!
COULD YOU POSSIBLY BE FIGHTING OVER OUR FAIR MAIDEN DANI?
YES!
OF COURSE NOT!
TICK
TOCK
TICK
TOCK
TICK
TOCK

JUST ONE SONG, OKAY?
O-OKAY.
TICK
TOCK
TICK
CRACK
TOCK
TICK
TOCK
TICK
WHAT'S THAT?
THEY'RE WITCHES, AREN'T THEY?
BOOM

THERE'S SO MANY OF THEM...
THEY AREN'T MOVING.
THEY CAME OUT OF NOWHERE!
NO, THEY'VE BEEN THERE—
THEY WERE JUST SUDDENLY VISIBLE AT MIDNIGHT.
WHAT ARE THEY DOING THERE?
JUST LIKE IN A FAIRY TALE.
THEY SURE LOOK LIKE THE VILLAINS OF A FAIRY TALE...
CAREFUL, EVERYONE! THEY BROUGHT DRAGONS!
THEY'RE ATTACKING THE VILLAGE!

QUICK, HIDE!
HUH?
TO ALL YOU WITCHES WHO ATTENDED THIS PARTY HOPING FOR A BRIGHTER FUTURE...
IT WAS A SETUP.
THEY TOOK AWAY YOUR WANDS AND CLOSED THE GATES OF THE PALACE TO YOU.
THE KING MAY LOOK HARMLESS,
BUT DON'T FORGET HE'S THE ONE WHO ORDERED THE BURNING OF WITCHES IN THE FIRST PLACE.
WHAT IS SHE TALKING ABOUT?
I SAW HER ON THE SABBATH—THAT'S MRS. WYTTE!
HER DRAGON JUST DESTROYED THE GUARD POST.
W
YOU'LL SOON UNDERSTAND THAT YOUR KING ONLY WISHES TO SEE YOU DEAD.

THAT LADY IS QUITE IMPRESSIVE...
SHE'S... SHE'S MY MOTHER, GUYS.
LET'S GET YOU AND DORIAN OUT OF HERE BEFORE SHE SEES YOU.
YES, THAT WOULD BE BEST.
DON'T WORRY, DANI, WE'VE GOT YOU COVERED.
WE SHOULD GO GET OUR WANDS, IN CASE WE NEED TO FIGHT.
I DON'T DO MAGIC ANYMORE.
ALSO, AGAINST WHOM ARE WE FIGHTING, ALEX?
WITCHES OR NON-MAGICAL PEOPLE?
WELL—
IT'S STILL NOT VERY CLEAR.
BUT WE HAVE TO DO SOMETHING.
WE CAN'T JUST WALK AWAY.
GREAT!
THIS WAS EASIER THAN EXPECTED.

WAY TOO EASY.
DON'T LET YOUR GUARD DOWN, HANS.
NOW, YOUR MAJESTY?
WAIT. LET MORE WITCHES ENTER THE PALACE.
WHAT ABOUT MONICA, DARLING? WHERE IS SHE?
UGH...
MONICA...
ARE YOU ALL RIGHT?
YES. BUT MY HAIR IS A MESS.
HAHAHA! YOU LOOK GREAT.
THAT EXPLOSION, THOUGH...
WHAT WAS IT?
AHA!
DORIAN, WAIT!

TAKE A PEEK, BUT STAY HIDDEN.
WHAT THE—
A DRAGON!
AND LOOK... YOUR FATHER!
WHAT IF HE SEES ME AND TURNS ME INTO THE KING OF WITCHES?
HE CAN'T.
HOW CAN YOU BE SO SURE?
DAMIEN WAS RIGHT, I'VE BEEN HIDING HORRIBLE SPELLS.
BUT YOU DIDN'T USE THEM ON ANYONE.
YOU'RE A GOOD PERSON.
NO, I'M NOT.
THERE'S SOMETHING I HAVEN'T TOLD YOU...
I SAW PRINCE WILLIAM.
HUH?
ON THE FLOATING ROCK.
I DIDN'T RECOGNIZE HIM AT FIRST.
BUT WHEN I DID, I LET HIM GO ANYWAYS.
NOW HE COULD BE DEAD... AND IT'D BE MY FAULT.
WHY WOULD YOU DO THAT, DORIAN?
BECAUSE I...

I THINK THAT I...
AAAAH!
PLEASE, HELP! THE FLOOR IS COLLAPSING!
OH NO, ANNE!
COME ON, DORIAN, WE HAVE TO DO SOMETHING!
WAIT!
DO YOU HATE ME, MONICA?
I DON'T KNOW.
YOU'VE DONE SOMETHING TERRIBLE.
BUT RIGHT NOW, I NEED YOUR HELP.
QUICK!
OKAY.

CHAPTER 31

SOMEBODY, PLEASE! HELP ME!
DAMN GIRL, YOU'RE HEAVY!
ATTACK THEM, HILDE. WE CAN'T LET THEM CATCH US.
THANK YOU FOR YOUR VALUABLE CONTRIBUTION, DEAR BROTHER.
I DON'T KNOW WHAT I WOULD DO WITHOUT YOU.
HURRY, DORIAN! CAST THAT SPELL YOU ALWAYS USE ON NICO.
WHICH ONE?
YOUR MAJESTY, WE'RE FIGHTING THEM OFF.
PERFECT.
YOUR MAJESTY! ARE YOU ALL RIGHT?!

DON'T WORRY, EVERYTHING IS UNDER CONTROL.
?
AIM INTO THE AIR—ON MY SIGNAL!
NOW!
WHAT THE...?
HOW?
PENDRAGON WARNED ME THAT THEY WOULD ATTACK WITH DRAGONS.
ICE SPELLS CAN BE USED TO WEAKEN THEM.
HE'S BEEN TRAINING MANY OF MY MEN.
THIS WAY THEY SHOULD BE ABLE TO DEFEAT THE DRAGON.
I COULDN'T ASK YOU TO FIGHT AGAINST YOUR OWN FAMILY, DAMIEN.

BUT NOW IT'S ALL OVER.
HANS AND HILDE WYTTE...
YOU'RE UNDER ARREST FOR ATTEMPTED—
GO TO HELL!
I GET IT. WE LOST.
AND NOW YOU'LL SENTENCE US TO DEATH BECAUSE WE'RE WITCHES!
DESPITE USING MAGIC TO YOUR OWN ADVANTAGE.
HYPOCRITE!
BURNING WITCHES HAS BEEN ILLEGAL FOR YEARS.
BUT I PLAN TO MAKE AN EXCEPTION FOR YOU.
NO!
YOUR MAJESTY, PLEASE...
THAT WOULD BE TOO MUCH. I—
DAMIEN, SON!
WE CAME HERE FOR YOU.
YOU ARE THE CHOSEN KING.
THE KING OF WITCHES!
TURN THEM ALL INTO FROGS. RELEASE THE DRAGON.
DO IT FOR ME!
SHUT UP!

DAMIEN,
COME BACK HERE!
I FEEL SICK.
THIS...IS A NIGHTMARE.
COUGH
COUGH
I DIDN'T WANT TO SEE THEM EVER AGAIN.
BUT...
I DON'T WANT THEM TO DIE, EITHER.
MOM?! W–
LONG TIME NO SEE, DAMIEN.
I'M HAPPY TO SEE YOU, SON.
WE WANT YOU TO BE THE NEW KING.
YES, BUT...
I DON'T WANT THAT. I JUST WANT TO LIVE IN PEACE.
BUT DAMIEN...
YOU OWE ME.
EVERYONE AT THE SABBATH HEARD THE PROPHECY.
THEY'LL ONLY FOLLOW US IF WE CROWN ONE OF OUR CHILDREN.
YOU STARTED ALL OF THIS.
IT'S RIGHT FOR YOU TO END IT.

AND SEEKING REVENGE FOR YOUR MOTHER IS THE BEST WAY TO DO THAT.
ISN'T THAT PRINCE WILLIAM'S SWORD?
DO YOU KNOW WHERE HE IS?
YES. HE'S ALIVE.
FOR NOW.
WILL YOU DO IT FOR YOUR MOTHER?
SO WHAT DO YOU SAY, DAMIEN?
WILL YOU BECOME...
THE KING OF WITCHES?
YES.
THAT'S HOW I'LL

PROTECT THEM ALL.
DAMIEN, WHAT ARE YOU DOING?
I'M SORRY, YOUR MAJESTY.

COME ON, DORIAN.
SOMEBODY HELP ALREADY...
SHE'S HEAVIER THAN SHE LOOKS!
I'M ABOUT TO DIE, YOU COULD BE A BIT NICER.
NOBODY'S GOING TO DIE.
DO SOMETHING!
WHAT DO YOU WANT ME TO DO?
OH!
I'VE GOT IT. COME ON, GRAB A ROCK.
HUH?
DO WHAT I DO.
TAKE THAT!
OUCH.
STUPID BRATS!
ARGH.
IT'S ALL ABOUT AIM, DORIAN!
I'M TRYING.

TEAMWORK!
I'M GONNA BORROW THIS.
BRATS...
HURRY, I CAN'T HOLD HER ANY LONGER...
MONICA!
CALM DOWN, GIRLS.
I'M COMING!
TAKE MY HAND.
THANK YOU! YOU SAVED ME.
THERE'S NO NEED TO THANK ME.
I THOUGHT I WAS GOING TO DIE.
I'LL ALWAYS PROTECT YOU!
PSST, PRINCESS!
IF I WERE YOU, I'D FIND A PLACE TO HIDE.
YOU DIDN'T LEAVE WITH THE OTHER GUESTS?
CURIOSITY GOT THE BEST OF ME, AND THEN IT WAS TOO LATE.
GOSSIPY AS ALWAYS.
GET IN HERE, MONICA!

YOU CAN SEE EVERYTHING THROUGH HERE.
THERE'S A DRAGON!
MONICA, THAT FLYING WAS SO IMPRESSIVE.
I—
LET ME SEE. HOW DID THEY CATCH A DRAGON?
MONICA—
DON'T THINK I FORGOT ABOUT WILL.
I FEEL LIKE I DON'T KNOW YOU ANYMORE.
...
I'M SORRY.
I INSTANTLY REGRETTED IT.
I DON'T KNOW IF I CAN TRUST YOU ANYMORE.
WHY WOULD YOU DO IT, ANYWAY?
WHY? WELL...
I DIDN'T THINK. JUST THE IDEA OF YOU GOING AWAY TERRIFIED ME.
LEAVING THE MASTER'S HOUSE... GOING BACK TO THE CASTLE.
PLUS, I KNOW IT'S DUMB, BUT...
I LIKE YOU.

WHAT DID YOU JUST SAY?!
ER...
SAY IT AGAIN.
FORGET IT. I'M SO SORRY.
STOP APOLOGIZING.
I DIDN'T SAY I DISLIKE YOU.
UH...
WHAT?
THAT'S IT.
WHAT ARE YOU TWO DOING UNDER HERE?
CAN'T YOU SEE WHAT'S HAPPENING?

SAY FAREWELL TO YOUR KING.
AND WELCOME THE KING OF WITCHES.
NO—
WAIT!
YOU CAN'T DO THAT.
WHY NOT? WE NEED THAT CROWN.
BEHEADING IS TOO EASY.
WE NEED TO SHOW HOW SUPERIOR WE ARE— EMBARRASS HIM.
DAMIEN—
YOU'LL BE MY PET.

YOU WON'T BE NEEDING THIS CROWN ANYMORE, YOUR MAJESTY.
OR YOUR CASTLE.
OR YOUR SERVANTS.
NOTHING BELONGS TO YOU.
IT BELONGS TO DAMIEN—
THE KING OF WITCHES.

CHAPTER 32

HURRY, THIS WAY!
WE LEFT THE WANDS AT THE ENTRANCE.
YOU WITCHES CAN'T PASS.
YOU'LL PAY FOR THIS!
OUCH.
HEY!
YOU'RE WRONG!
WE'RE THE GOOD ONES.
THERE ARE NO GOOD WITCHES!
WE LET YOU IN OUR CITY
AND YOU ATTACKED US.
WE NEED OUR WANDS TO SAVE DORIAN.
GET OUT OF MY WAY, IDIOTS!

NICO?!
THAT'S DANGEROUS!
ARGH!
THANK YOU, GUYS!
GOOD DISTRACTION.
DANI!
YOU'LL SPEND A LOVELY NIGHT IN JAIL...
DON'T LET HER GET AWAY.
HA!
COME ON, DANI!
THE WANDS ARE THIS WAY.
HA HA HA!

THE CITY HAS BEEN TAKEN!
IT LOOKS LIKE THE KING...
GET OUT, QUICKLY!
SAVE YOURSELVES.
DID YOU FIND ANYTHING, DANI?
NOTHING YET!
AH! BINGO!
HERE YOU GO.
YOU FOUND IT.
I'LL KEEP LOOKING.

THE KING IS DEAD.
KILLED BY WITCHES...
NO, YOU TAKE IT, ALEX.
I'M NOT DOING MAGIC ANYMORE.
WHY NOT?
JUST MAKING SURE I'M ON THE GOOD SIDE, I SUPPOSE...
WHAT DO YOU MEAN? WE'LL ONLY USE OUR MAGIC TO HELP PEOPLE!
KEEP IT.
DOING MAGIC DOESN'T MAKE YOU A BAD PER—!

THAT'S FOR THE KING.
BLOOD FOR BLOOD, WITCHES.
HEY, KID!
DROP THE WAND.

SORRY YOU HAD TO SEE THAT, KID.
BUT ALL WITCHES HAVE TO GO.
WHAT THE—?
IT CAN'T BE...
NO!
ALEX!
SO ALEX...
...DESERVED TO DIE?

SHE DESERVED TO DIE?!
UGH!
L-LET ME GO!
LET ME GO, WITCH!
WHAT'S GOING ON?
SHE PUT A SPELL ON HIM!
YOU'RE ALL A THREAT TO SOCIETY!
THAT'S NOT TRUE.
LIAR.
UGH...

NOT ALL OF US ARE EVIL.
WE'RE NOT A THREAT.
I'VE MET CHARMING WITCHES.
GOOD, LOVELY, PEACEFUL WITCHES.
ABSOLUTELY BRILLIANT WITCHES.
BUT YOU JUDGE US.
AND FEAR US.
YOU PERSECUTE US.
YOU BURN US.

IS THIS THE GAME YOU WANT TO PLAY?
WELL, THEN...
LET'S PLAY!
IT'S ALWAYS LIKE THIS...
MY MAGIC AND MY FEELINGS MIX UP.
THEY BLEND INTO ONE ANOTHER.
THE DARKER MY FEELINGS ARE,
THE MORE POWERFUL MY MAGIC IS.
AND RIGHT NOW,
MY FEELINGS
ARE DARKER THAN EVER.

DANI? HOW...?
HOW IS SHE DOING ALL OF THIS?
AND WITH NO WAND?
IS SHE...?
DOES THIS MEAN SHE...?
DANI!
STOP!

UGH...
DON'T LET ANYBODY SEE YOU LIKE THAT EVER AGAIN!
NICO...
THEY KILLED...
ALEX IS...
I KNOW.
UH...
BUT WHY?
I DON'T UNDERSTAND...

NICO, WHAT ARE YOU DOING?
NOTHING...
WHAT HAPPENED?
ARE YOU OKAY, DANI?
NO.
NOT ANYMORE.

CHAPTER 33

THIS FEELS LIKE A DREAM...
OR MAYBE A NIGHTMARE.
I COULD HAVE FOUGHT.
THERE'S ONLY ONE BROOM.
WHAT SHOULD WE DO?
THE PALACE IS SURROUNDED.
DO WE JUMP?
STEP
STEP
SOMEONE'S COMING!
GET BEHIND ME!
BUT I THINK...
STEP

I TRUST DAMIEN.
IT'S DAMIEN.
YOU'RE A TRAITOR!
LET US GO, PLEASE...
MAYBE THAT WAS THE BLACK HAIR THE MASTER SAW.
LOOK, AN OPEN DOOR!
THE KING IS THERE.
EXCEPT THAT DAMIEN'S EYES...
MAYBE THE KING OF WITCHES FOUND THE PRINCESS.
HIS EYES ARE STILL ICY BLUE.

YOUR MAJESTY?
NOTHING. KEEP LOOKING.
YES, YOUR MAJESTY.
POW
A FLYING FROG!
CARLO!
WHAT'S NEXT?
AND HE BROUGHT YOUR WAND.
NOW WE JUST NEED A WAY FOR ALL OF US TO GET OUT OF HERE...
DORIAN, I'VE GOT AN IDEA.
THIS IS AWESOME!
DANI! OVER HERE!
EVERYONE'S OKAY!

GUYS, OVER HERE!
HANG ON A SECOND, DANI. I NEED TO TALK TO YOU.
LET ME GO, NICO.
WAIT!
LET'S GO HOME, DORIAN.

ARE YOU OKAY, MONICA?
NO.
ALL OF THIS IS HORRIBLE. I CAN'T PICTURE IT GOING ANY WORSE.
TRUE.
I THINK DANI'S AVOIDING ME.
BECAUSE SHE FOUND OUT AS WELL.
FOUND OUT ABOUT WHAT?
...
NICO?
IT'S ABOUT HER.
?
CONSIDERING EVERYTHING TODAY, I'M ALMOST SURE...
I THINK SHE WILL BE
THE QUEEN OF WITCHES.

HOOKY

• EXTRAS •

23.5
...
OKAY, YOU CAN DO THIS.
DANI!
HEY, DANI, WAKE UP!
I HAVE TO ASK YOU SOMETHING!
IT'S IMPORTA—!
AH!
ARGH, A COCKROACH!
IT'S ME, NICO!
HOW DARE YOU?!
GO BACK TO YOUR ROOM!
I WAS THINKING...
DORIAN SAID THAT WITCHES ARE SUPPOSED TO WEAR BLACK CLOTHES, RIGHT?
DO YOU THINK I WOULD BE ABLE TO PERFORM MAGIC IF I DRESSED AS A PROPER WITCH?
CLOTHES ARE JUST CLOTHES, NICO.

COME ON, DANI!
YOU'RE LITERALLY WEARING THE MOST COLORFUL PAJAMAS ON PURPOSE.
WILL YOU HELP ME OR NOT?!
HUH, WELL...
OKAY. BUT I THINK THAT WE SHOULD ASK MONICA FOR ADVICE.
FINE. BUT DON'T TELL ANYONE OTHER THAN HER.
ESPECIALLY NOT YOUR BROTHER.
THE NEXT MORNING...
OF COURSE I'LL HELP YOU.
I LOVE DRESSING UP MY DOLLS.
I'M NOT A DOLL!
BUT DORIAN IS THE EXPERT ON WITCH ETIQUETTE.
TOO BAD HE'S BUSY RIGHT NOW.
I TOLD HIM THAT THERE APPEAR TO BE ENCHANTED CREATURES IN THE SWAMP.
YOU KNOW HE LOVES ANIMALS AND DISCOVERING NEW SPELLS.
I BET HE'S KISSING TOADS RIGHT NOW.

DON'T WORRY.
WITH MY NATURAL TALENT AND OBSERVATIONAL ABILITIES, WE'LL BRING OUT THE WITCH IN YOU.
YOU'VE GOT TO BE KIDDING.
I'M NOT GOING TO DRESS LIKE THAT WEIRDO.
YOU DON'T LIKE IT?
THEN MAYBE—
NO!
NOW I LOOK LIKE DANI!
YOU'RE VERY PICKY! LET'S SEE...
TRY A CLASSIC LOOK.
PRINCESS...
I LOOK RIDICULOUS.
SIGH...
OKAY, THEN...

WHAT ABOUT THIS?
I TOOK INSPIRATION FROM ALEX'S OUTFIT.
I LOOK COOL. I LIKE IT.
OH.
GUYS!
I'VE DISCOVERED SOMETHING AMAZING!
DORIAN.
I HAVEN'T FOUND ANYONE TRANSFORMED INTO A TOAD, BUT...
I TURNED CARLO...
...INTO A PERSON! (KIND OF.)
WHOAA!
HE LOOKS ADORABLE!
EWW...
HE LOOKS DISGUSTING.
COULDN'T YOU USE YOUR FREE TIME TO FIND A WAY TO RETURN ME TO MY ORIGINAL SIZE?
N-NICO, YOU...
YOU LOOK SUPER COOL!
ARE YOU DRESSED AS A WITCH?!
YES! WHAT ABOUT IT?!
I DIDN'T ASK FOR YOUR OPINION.

AH!
DORIAN?
HE SEEMS UPSET.
HMPH.
WHY ARE YOU SO RUDE TO HIM?
HERE I AM AGAIN.
WHAT DO YOU THINK?
WHOAAA!
THIS... THIS IS...
YOU LOOK SO COOL, DORIAN!
THIS IS SPLENDID!
THANK YOU.
WOW, PRINCESS. DON'T TELL ME YOU LIKE DOR—
OF COURSE NOT, YOU FOOL!
WHAT'S HAPPENING NOW IS KNOWN AS THE "BAD-BOY EFFECT."
ANY BOY, NO MATTER HOW SILLY HE IS IN REALITY, IS CAPABLE OF SEEMING SUPER COOL AND MATURE BY WEARING A BAD-BOY OUTFIT.
INTERESTING.
OH, NOW I GET IT...
THE END

27.5
ENOUGH ALREADY, NICO!
STOP DISTRACTING DORIAN. WE'RE TRYING TO STUDY.
A LITTLE LEVITATION SPELL ISN'T TOO MUCH TO ASK OF THE GREAT PROFESSOR WYTTE, IS IT?
YOU STILL CAN'T BEAT ME.
YOU WANT TO BET?
HEY, GUYS!
ME AND SOME FRIENDS ARE GOING STARGAZING TONIGHT. WANNA JOIN OR ARE YOU BUSY?
YES!
I MEAN...NO! WE HAVE ABSOLUTELY NO PLANS. I'M COMPLETELY FREE.
WHAT A CRAPPY SPELL, DORIAN! LEARN HOW TO DO MAGIC!
AND YOU, MARK, GET LOST.
IT WOULD BE SO COOL IF YOU CAME TOO, NICO.
NO WAY.
DANI ISN'T GOING ANYWHERE!
IT'S LATE!
PARTY POOPER.

I'M SICK OF DANI AND MARK HANGING OUT ALL THE TIME.
DON'T TAKE IT TOO HARD...
I'M SURE MARK WAS ABOUT TO INVITE YOU AS WELL.
HE REALLY LIKES YOU.
IT'S NOT THAT.
I'M JUST TIRED OF DANI'S OBSESSION WITH THAT BOY.
WE'RE STILL KIDS. IT'S TOO SOON FOR A ROMANCE.
PEOPLE LOSE THEIR HEADS WHEN IT COMES TO LOVE.
THAT'S WHAT YOU THINK...?
REALLY?
ARGH!
I FORGOT THAT MONICA'S WHOLE LIFE REVOLVES AROUND ROMANCE.
I'M TELLING THE SELF-PROCLAIMED EXPERT ON ROMANCE THAT LOVE IS SILLY!
I'M THE ONE WHO'S LOST MY HEAD!
BUT I WAS TALKING ABOUT DANI AND ME... YOU'RE OLDER. MUCH OLDER!
MUCH OLDER?
OF COURSE.
YOU HAVE A FIANCÉ...
I'M SURE YOU'VE EVEN HAD YOUR FIRST KISS.
YOU'RE WRONG!

I MEAN... WILLIAM DID TRY TO KISS ME SEVERAL TIMES.
BUT HE ALWAYS CHOSE THE MOST INAPPROPRIATE MOMENTS.
AND THE TRUTH IS...
...HE ALSO TRIED TO KISS OTHER PEOPLE.
NEEDLESS TO SAY, HE GOT REJECTED. A LOT.
HE IS COMPLETELY INCAPABLE OF READING THE ATMOSPHERE AND BEING ROMANTIC.
IS THAT SO?
IT'S OBVIOUS THAT HE'S NEVER READ A ROMANCE NOVEL!
ON THE OTHER HAND, I AM A COMPLETE EXPERT ON THIS MATTER.
THAT'S GOOD TO HEAR.

THAT MEANS WHEN THE TIME COMES...
YOU'LL BE ABLE TO READ THE ATMOSPHERE.
I'M SURE THE MOMENT OF YOUR FIRST KISS— WHENEVER THAT IS—
WILL BE PERFECTLY ROMANTIC.
WHAT ARE YOU STUDYING?
POTIONS!
WHAT DO YOU WANT?
I THOUGHT WE COULD STARGAZE FROM HERE.
I BROUGHT BANANA BREAD!
YAY! SLEEPOVER PARTY!
LATER THAT NIGHT...
WHAT WAS THAT?
I MUST BRUSH UP ON MY KNOWLEDGE.
A TRUE INTELLECTUAL MUST KNOW ABOUT ALL SUBJECTS.
THIS IS FOR THE SAKE OF SCIENCE, ABSOLUTELY.
THE END